"I've Waited Long Enough," Marek Said. "What's Your Answer? Will You Marry Me?"

Her insides roiled and her palms became damp even though her hands felt icy as she gazed into his brown eyes.

Taking a deep breath, she nodded. "Yes, I will."

He closed his eyes briefly, then opened them. He pulled her up and gave her a light hug. "Thank you," he said in a voice that sounded choked with emotion.

He smelled of citrus and sandalwood and the fresh cottony scent of his immaculate dress shirt. He was warm, tall and his arms around her felt reassuring. He leaned away a fraction to look down at her and her only thought at that moment was how handsome he was. "We'll make this work, Camille," he said in a husky voice.

A pang racked her because his emotional reaction was not due to her, but to her baby. "I don't want to fall in love," she whispered, biting back the words that if she did, he would break her heart.

Dear Reader,

The Texan's Contract Marriage is a story about the blazing love affair of a cosmopolitan rising opera star and a sophisticated Texan billionaire who is a cowboy at heart.

Here are two people who, out of love, put a baby first in their lives and end up finding love themselves. Their story is about the unselfishness and blessings of love filling lives.

Also, through this story, I could express my great love of music, of Texas and the West. In this story you will meet a woman who brings a man out of his grief over the terrible loss of his fiancée and his brother.

Marek and Camille unselfishly do what is best for Noah and when they do, they find their own lives blessed. They prove that love can conquer all. Thank you for selecting this book.

Sara Orwig

SARA ORWIG

THE TEXAN'S CONTRACT MARRIAGE

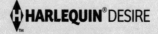

HARLEQUIN®DESIRE

Recycling programs
for this product may
not exist in your area.

ISBN-13: 978-0-373-73242-5

THE TEXAN'S CONTRACT MARRIAGE

Copyright © 2013 by Sara Orwig

Printed in U.S.A.

Books by Sara Orwig

Harlequin Desire

**Texas-Sized Temptation #2086
**A Lone Star Love Affair #2098
**Wild Western Nights #2110
§Relentless Pursuit #2159
§The Reluctant Heiress #2176
§Midnight Under the Mistletoe #2195
The Texan's Contract Marriage #2229

Silhouette Desire

Falcon's Lair #938
The Bride's Choice #1019
A Baby for Mommy #1060
Babes in Arms #1094
Her Torrid Temporary
  Marriage #1125
The Consummate Cowboy #1164
The Cowboy's Seductive
  Proposal #1192
World's Most Eligible Texan #1346
Cowboy's Secret Child #1368
The Playboy Meets
  His Match #1438
Cowboy's Special Woman #1449
††Do You Take This Enemy? #1476
††The Rancher, the Baby
  & the Nanny #1486
Entangled with a Texan #1547
*Shut Up and Kiss Me #1581
*Standing Outside the Fire #1594
Estate Affair #1657
†Pregnant with the First Heir #1752

†Revenge of the
  Second Son #1757
†Scandals from the
  Third Bride #1762
Seduced by the
  Wealthy Playboy #1813
‡Pregnant at the Wedding #1864
‡Seduced by the Enemy #1875
‡Wed to the Texan #1887
**Dakota Daddy #1936
**Montana Mistress #1941
**Wyoming Wedding #1947
Tempting the
  Texas Tycoon #1989
Marrying the Lone Star
  Maverick #1997
**Texas Tycoon's Christmas
  Fiancée #2049

††Stallion Pass
*Stallion Pass: Texas Knights
†The Wealthy Ransomes
‡Platinum Grooms
**Stetsons & CEOs
§Lone Star Legacy

Other titles by this author
available in ebook format

SARA ORWIG

lives in Oklahoma. She has a patient husband who will take her on research trips anywhere from big cities to old forts. She is an avid collector of Western history books. With a master's degree in English, Sara has written historical romance, mainstream fiction and contemporary romance. Books are beloved treasures that take Sara to magical worlds, and she loves both reading and writing them.

To David with love

One

Marek Rangel glanced at his watch and pushed aside the papers in front of him. It was the morning of the second day of April, a sunny, spring day. Two minutes until his appointment with the opera singer. He had no idea why Camille Avanole had requested to meet with him or even how she had gotten through to his private line. He didn't attend the opera and it wasn't on the list of charities of his family's foundation. He had been tempted to refuse to see her, but, out of courtesy, he had decided he would meet her briefly.

He gazed around his corner office on the twenty-second floor in the building that was headquarters for his company, Rangel Energy, Inc. His secretary was to interrupt them if Ms. Avanole ran over the allotted thirty minutes he had agreed upon.

A light knock on the door brought him to his feet.

His secretary thrust her head into the room. "Camille Avanole is here."

"Tell her to come in," he said, stepping away from his oversize antique mahogany desk.

A vivacious black-haired woman approached him with her hand extended. A smile revealed white, perfect teeth; she had a sparkle in her enormous, thickly lashed blue eyes. The plain black dress she wore with a black scarf wrapped casually below her neck was striking. She had an inviting presence, as if she were about to share a delightful surprise. Suddenly, Marek's interest stirred.

"Mr. Rangel," she said. "I'm Camille Avanole."

Her warm hand was soft, yet her handshake was firm. At the moment of contact, he was jolted by an electric response, an intense awareness that he had not felt with any woman since he had lost his fiancée. Realizing he was staring, he released her hand.

"Please have a seat."

Marek focused on her interesting walk. As she crossed the room, he noticed her tiny waist. Her beauty had to be an asset to her career.

"Just call me Marek," he said, certain this meeting would be brief and he would never see her again.

Two antique velvet wingback chairs stood in front of the mahogany desk. Marek sat down facing her. She crossed long, shapely legs that had to be the best-looking legs on the opera circuit.

"Are you in Dallas for a performance or is this your home?" he asked politely, noticing she had the largest eyes he had ever seen. Striking, spellbinding eyes.

"I'm back in Dallas this spring for a performance I'll have soon."

He had the feeling of being studied as intently as a bug under a microscope.

"So what is the mysterious reason you wanted to see me that we couldn't discuss on the phone?"

Her smile vanished and she straightened. He could add the word *compelling* to his description of her. He couldn't imagine her playing any part on stage except the star; she would steal the show even in the background. Even while sitting still, she exuded energy.

"You lost your brother and your fiancée a year ago this March. I'm sorry for your loss," she said.

"Thank you," he replied stiffly, waiting and wondering why she had brought that up.

"I knew your brother," she said quietly.

Surprised, he focused on her. "How's that?"

"We met at a New Year's Eve party. You had a very charming brother."

"Yes, Kern was charismatic, fun," Marek said, his mind racing. Had she and Kern secretly married? He dismissed that notion immediately. Kern would have told him. "Let's cut to the chase here. What does your knowing my brother have to do with your asking for an appointment to talk to me?"

"I'm going to give you a shock and I'm trying to lead into it instead of just hitting you with it all at once."

"At this point, I'm ready for you to hit me with it," he said, unable to fathom what she might be about to tell him.

She pulled out a picture to show him. He looked at a baby boy with big dark eyes who was smiling. Marek's breath left him as if he had received a blow to his midsection. The picture looked like dozens he had seen at his parents' home. The baby had big brown eyes like his brother, tangled black hair, the same color his brother's had been, the same color as his own. Marek looked up. "Who is he?"

"I think you already know," Camille answered quietly. "He's my son. Your brother was his father."

Even though that was what he had already guessed, it was another hard blow to his midsection to hear her declare it.

"I can see a resemblance, but Kern would have told me. I'm sorry, I find this difficult to believe. It could be a coincidence he looks like my brother. How old is this child?"

"He's six months old now. Noah was born October 4, last year."

"Six months old," Marek repeated, dazed. He stared at the picture in disbelief, an icy chill setting in as he wondered if this was a play for money. "Kern never said a word about knowing you. He would have said something to me."

"We met at a New Year's Eve party over a year ago," she said in her silky soprano voice. "Kern charmed me. We had mutual friends, so I felt safe leaving with him. It was an exception in my very structured life—two nights of passion that I'd never had before and never since. We used protection, but I still got pregnant. I've managed to keep the publicity low-key. It hasn't been difficult to keep the baby out of the spotlight. An opera performer—at least at my current level—is not the same as a movie star. I have only recently had more success and more fame."

"I find it difficult to believe this baby really is Kern's."

"He is. You can have a paternity test. The DNA should give you an answer."

Marek could not stop looking at the picture of the baby. "What's his name?"

"Noah Avanole."

"I'm still amazed Kern didn't tell me."

"He said he was going to tell you, but he probably never had the chance."

"You're right." Unable to sit still, Marek stood and walked to the window to stare at the picture while questions raced through his thoughts. "Kern had a baby. How long before the flight did he know?" Marek asked.

"The evening before he left I told Kern I was pregnant, so he didn't know until the day before the plane crash."

Marek drew a deep breath. "Was this on his mind when he flew to Denver?"

"I'm sure it was," she answered.

Marek felt as if he had had another blow. A year ago in March, his brother had had a flight to a horse sale in Kansas City. Marek had intended to fly to Denver to pick up his fiancée, who had been there for a wedding. Instead, Kern had offered to pick her up after leaving Kansas City. On the way home they had been caught in an unexpected storm. When the plane had crashed, both had been killed. Now he wondered how much his brother's thoughts and attention had been distracted by the news from Camille. Marek continued staring at the baby's picture. He remembered Camille and turned to find her sitting quietly.

"Thank you for telling me," Marek said, crossing the room. "I'll think about the paternity test. Since you're telling me now, I assume you want me to do something. We might as well get to the point of this meeting."

"I've had time to think about this. I can support Noah. What I want is for Noah to know the Rangels. Kern was such a cowboy. I want Noah to have an appreciation for ranching, so he will understand his father better. I think he should know his father's family."

Marek had received one surprise after another. If she really didn't want money, he would be shocked. He figured this was a ploy to get him to let down his guard.

"I'll have to think about this and talk to my attorney."

She smiled. "I hope you don't need an attorney. I felt you should know, and there was no good way to tell you on the phone or by email. Even in person, it's a shock. But what's done is done."

"The crash was a year ago last month. Why did you wait until now to tell me?"

"I was busy caring for Noah and undecided what to do.

I was away from Dallas, and I wanted to tell you in person. I knew I would be back. Also, it's given me time to really think this through. You could help by being a father figure for your nephew, too."

Marek drew a deep breath at the thought of the responsibility she wanted him to take. Yet if this baby was Kern's, a part of Kern, Marek wanted to know him and watch him grow up. A part of Kern—the thought twisted his insides. He looked at the picture again. Why hadn't Kern told him? He probably had planned to when he returned from the flight.

"Kern never knew this baby. You'll take good care of him. Maybe it would be better if I just stepped back out of the way," Marek said stiffly. He still harbored a kernel of doubt that this was Kern's baby and expected her to make an effort to pull him back into being part of the baby's life.

"I hope you'll come see him. Of course, what you do now is your choice. And I'll take the best care of him I possibly can. If you ever want to see him, you'll be able to contact me."

"That's good to hear. Do you have parents who are living?"

"Yes. My parents live in Saint Louis." She smiled, remaining poised. "Your brother told me how different the two of you were. I supposed I'd hoped you would react the way Kern did, but you're not Kern."

She reached into her purse to withdraw a piece of paper. She held it out to him. "Your brother sent me an email, and I printed it out. This is a copy of it. I've made an effort to preserve it for Noah."

For the first time, Marek began to believe what she had told him. He was reluctant to read the email. He was certain his life was about to take another unexpected turn. Drawing a deep breath, Marek quickly scanned the message.

Camille:
  When I return from Denver, we'll go to dinner. I want to be with you when Noah is born. Perfect name. I can't get used to the fact that I'm going to be a dad. Super-mega-duper! I'm overwhelmed, overjoyed. I want to be a big part of his life. Already love him. I want to be with you. My deepest gratitude for telling me. I'll call tomorrow night. We didn't plan this. Miracles happen. I'm overjoyed.
  Kern

  Marek felt weak in the knees. This was Kern's message. Marek looked up at Camille, who gazed back steadily. He was certain now that she had given birth to Kern's baby. There was another Rangel in the world. Until this moment, Marek hadn't fully believed the baby was Kern's. Now he couldn't doubt it.

  Marek felt another tight squeeze to his chest, this time as if his heart had been grabbed by a giant fist. He missed Kern terribly, and this brought back all the incredible pain of his loss. With thoughts of Kern came remembrance of Jillian. He hated the knot in his throat. Making an effort, he struggled to get his emotions under control before he looked up or spoke. Finally, he raised his head and handed back the letter.

  "That definitely sounds like my brother. Super-mega-duper—one of his favorite expressions. Thank you for showing me the message."

  "That's fine. That's a copy. If you want it, keep it."

  "Thanks," he said, dropping the paper on his desk. "I'll take it to show my sister. I would like a paternity test just to settle any questions that would ever arise. This is Kern's baby. That message is Kern talking. There's no mistake."

  Smiling, looking happier, she nodded. "We can do a paternity test. I expected you to request one."

  "This has been almost as big a shock as if you told me I

have a son. My brother and I were close. I assume you haven't contacted my sister because I would have heard from her."

"No, I didn't because in what little time we were together, your brother talked far more about you."

"She's seven years older than I am. Kern and I were closer, but she'll want to know about Noah."

"If you and your sister decide you want to see him, we can arrange that."

He nodded. He felt as if his breath had been knocked out of him. He needed to think about the baby and make decisions about what he wanted to do.

"You won't always live in Dallas, will you?" he asked.

"I've only been in Texas three times in my life. I'll leave here the end of June. I'll be singing in New Mexico in August, so I'll stay there."

"And you'll take the baby with you."

"Yes, of course, but I still hope that he can get to know you and your family as he grows. If he does, you would be a good father figure for him, I'm sure. Kern would have been a wonderful one."

"You could have gone on with your life and never told me," Marek said, looking into her wide crystal-blue eyes. "There's no way I would have found out. Now you'll have to share Noah."

She studied him intently. "It wouldn't have been right. I couldn't do it. I thought about doing that because it would have been infinitely easier, but I love Noah and want what's best for him. The day will come when he'll want to know his father. Since he can't do that, he will want to know his father's family. I truly think you'll be a good influence. The ranching aspect has to be good for a growing boy. If he gets to know you and know ranching, I'll feel as if he knows part of his father."

"I agree with that, and I'm glad you made that decision,"

Marek said in a tight voice, trying to control his emotional reaction to her statement. "Will you be in town if I want to get in touch with you?"

"Yes. In June I perform here in Dallas. Then in July I'll go to Santa Fe for my August performance. After that I'll go home to Saint Louis through September so I can be with my family. I have a voice teacher here in Dallas that I like very much, so I may be in Texas more often than I have been in the past."

"You have a busy schedule. Thank you for calling me. You didn't have to share with us at all," he said again, still amazed she had done so.

"At first I was shocked by the news of my pregnancy. I thought it would end my career, and I was torn up over trying to figure out what to do. I felt uncertain about telling him. We only knew each other that one weekend. But the more I thought about it, the more I wanted Kern and the Rangels to be part of my baby's life."

As she walked to the door, Marek accompanied her. When she paused, he turned to face her, once again briefly caught in the blue of her eyes. She was a beautiful woman, and he understood why his brother had been attracted to her. "I'll talk to my sister. Also, I'll let my parents know. Thank you again for telling me," Marek said.

"I'm sorry for both your losses, your brother and your fiancée."

"Thank you," he replied stiffly. "I'll be in touch after I've talked to my sister."

She nodded. "I'm glad to have finally met you and glad you know about Noah. I'm sure I'll hear from you."

He watched her walk away and turned to go back into his office with his thoughts swirling. How much had Kern had his mind on the fact that he was going to be a father instead of concentrating on his flying? Had that news been a factor in Kern's crash?

And another baby in the family, and this time not only a little boy, but Kern's baby. He thought how delightful his two little nieces were. Now they would have the girls and Kern's little boy.

Marek canceled his appointments and called his pilot to fly back to the ranch to talk to the person he had been close to all his life.

Two hours later, Marek stood in the barn while his ranch foreman repaired a stall. Jess Grayson had pushed his battered, wide-brimmed brown hat back on his head and had his sleeves rolled high. While Jess drove in a nail, Marek held a board in place. "You can have a paternity test even with Kern gone."

"I know I can and I will, but I don't need to. That message is Kern's. It sounds like him. The baby looks like him. I've asked for a paternity test just to be sure."

"Good. So what are you going to do? Have you told Ginny?"

"Not yet. Wanted to talk to you first," he said, looking at Jess's weathered skin, which was the color of cowhide except for a pale band below his hairline where his hat shaded his skin from the sun.

"Ginny's family. I'm not."

"You might as well be. Your opinion still counts. I was all set to walk out of there and never look back when she pulled out Kern's message. I want you to read it when you finish nailing this board."

As soon as the board was in place, Marek fished the paper out of his pocket, unfolded it and handed it to Jess.

After a moment Jess looked up to meet Marek's gaze.

"Super-mega-duper," Jess repeated. "That's Kern." He shook his head as he returned the paper. "An opera star."

"A rising one. I don't know if she's a star yet. At this point, I don't know anything about her. Except I'm sure she's telling the truth about the baby."

"You really think she's not after money?" Jess asked, picking up another board and setting it in place below the first one. Marek stepped closer to help.

"She doesn't act like she is. Doesn't matter, really. Since I know this is Kern's baby, I can't walk away. He wouldn't if this were my baby, and I can't with Kern's."

"Even if he didn't love the lady?"

"Even if. Besides, you read that message. I would bet the ranch Kern was running through his mind how he could get her to marry him."

"Might be right. So you want this baby in the family?"

Watching Jess hammer, Marek thought a long time. "Yes, I do. Suppose he's a lot like Kern or even a little like Kern? It would drive me nuts to think a little boy was out there, Kern's son, who looked and acted like Kern and we didn't know him and didn't care. I can't do that. She wants us in his life. She wants him to have an appreciation for ranching. I can't argue against either of those."

"Then you've made your decision. Tell Ginny."

"I guess I have to."

"Frankly, I'd kind of like to see the little fellow myself."

"I'll call Ginny and then I'll call Camille and see if I can arrange to see her again, which will be easy to do. Per Kern's usual taste, she's a beauty," he said, remembering his first impression of her. "Also, she said she'd like me to be a father figure for Noah."

"That may be difficult if she doesn't live around here."

"True. She's leaving Dallas in July and going to Santa

Fe. She has a busy schedule. Until then, I'd like to know this child."

"Have you called your parents?"

Marek nodded. "I'm going to call to tell them. I want this baby to know the Rangels and us to know him. I'll go call Ginny. Thanks, Jess."

"You might get a little bit of Kern back," Jess said somberly.

"I'd like that, Jess, but I'm scared that's too much to hope for. I'll let you know what she says." Marek jogged to the house and inside, letting the door swing shut behind him.

While he called his sister, he remembered Camille—her vivid looks, her energetic presence. Good genes with Kern's genes. Should be a good combination. He talked for ten minutes, chatting briefly with each of his little nieces before his sister returned to the phone.

"Ginny, I have some news that will shock you. I can come back to Dallas to tell you or I can tell you on the phone, but you're in for a giant shock."

"You have to tell me now, Marek. Good grief, after that I can't wait for you to get to Dallas. What is it?"

"Do you know who Camille Avanole is?"

There was a moment's silence. "I don't think so. I can't think of a single Camille I know."

"Do you recognize the name?"

"If you don't tell me what you're getting at, Marek, I'm going to reach through this phone and grab you."

"Ginny, she called me and said she wanted to talk to me," he said, recalling the sparks he'd felt when they had touched while shaking hands—something he hadn't felt with a woman since the loss of Jillian. "She knew Kern," he continued. "Camille and Kern went out on a weekend over a year and a half ago. She got pregnant with Kern's baby."

"Kern had a baby?" Ginny's voice sounded faint and breathless.

"Yes, he did. He found out she was pregnant the day before he flew to Denver."

"Oh, my word. Do you suppose that's why he lost control and crashed? Was he thinking about the baby? Is it really Kern's? Maybe it's not and this is one of those women who try to take advantage—"

"Ginny," Marek stated firmly. "Listen to me. She has a note Kern sent her right before the flight. It's Kern's message. It sounds like him. She gave me a copy of it, and I'll show it to you."

"Marek, I do need to sit. This is a shock. A baby."

"A little boy named Noah. He's six months old. I have dinner with Camille tomorrow night to talk about the future," he said, realizing he was looking forward to seeing her again. Another first since losing Jillian. Maybe the numbness was wearing away. Or maybe it was Camille's beauty and captivating presence that had stirred his reactions. "I can't turn my back on that baby. I know he's Kern's son. She had a picture, and he looks like Kern."

"We have to know this little boy. Will she let us? Is she famous? You asked if I know her."

"She's in opera. I've looked her up. She's young. Only twenty-five. Her résumé is impressive to me," he said, thinking her looks were just as impressive.

"Opera? How did she get with Kern?"

"A New Year's Eve party where they had mutual friends."

"No wonder I didn't recognize the name. I'm country. What are you going to do?"

"I don't know. I'm thinking about options. I'll let you know."

"We have to keep this baby in our lives. If he's Kern's baby, we can't cut him out. Does she live in Texas?"

"No. She'll leave in July and take him with her."

"Have you told Jess?"

"Yes. He'd like to see the baby, too. I guess we're all hoping for a bit of Kern in our lives again."

"Wouldn't that be wonderful? You've given me a shock. You better break it gently to Mom and Dad."

"I will. I'll call Camille and see what I can set up to see him. I'll let you know. We'll both see him, I promise you."

He told her goodbye and called his parents, spending the next half hour breaking the news to them and catching up on their news.

Finished with family calls, he phoned Camille. In minutes he had plans to pick Camille up the next day and take her to Houston for dinner.

"You're not going out with him," Stephanie Avanole said, glaring at her sister.

"Yes, I am. I've given this a lot of thought. We've talked about it. He's Noah's relative," Camille replied, wiping her forehead and the back of her neck as she walked away from the treadmill. "I know you don't feel the way I do about this, but I think the Rangels have a right to see their nephew."

"They'll want to take him from you or tell you what to do with him. They're not going to ignore him. These are wealthy, powerful people, accustomed to getting their way. You said Kern said his older brother ran the family after he was grown. That he was much more serious than Kern."

"Tomorrow night Marek Rangel can talk and I'll listen. Stephanie, he's had a terrible loss and this is a shock."

"I still say you'll be sorry. You should never have told them about Noah, much less have agreed to go out with Marek Rangel tomorrow night. He's a tough cowboy and tougher businessman. I've heard a few people talk. He's had big losses—his fiancée as well as his only brother. He doesn't sound like the lighthearted, I-don't-care type."

"I had to tell him."

"I'm warning you," Stephanie said, frowning and placing her hands on her hips, "you'll regret this day. Marek Rangel will want to be part of Noah's life."

"I think he's entitled to be. I don't think he's any threat to me at all."

"You'll never convince me that this is good."

"Then you have a closed mind about it. He's not an ogre," Camille replied, remembering a handsome man with troubled brown eyes, a man who appeared hard, closed in a shell, inscrutable and preoccupied. A man who was nothing like his charming, devil-may-care brother.

Late afternoon Wednesday she dressed carefully in a deep blue dress with a vee neckline and long sleeves. Hoping to look successful, attractive and poised, she twisted and combed her hair to one side of her head, fastening it with a blue scarf. She had butterflies in the pit of her stomach and she didn't know why, unless deep down, she was more worried about what Marek might want than she had told her sister.

The moment he arrived at her house, dressed in a navy suit, a white Stetson and boots, he looked like the successful Texas rancher that he was. He also appeared powerful, commanding and threatening to her future. Stephanie's warnings haunted her.

In spite of the veiled look on his face, he was handsome enough to cause a jump in her pulse. For a fleeting moment she had a jittery dance of nerves and wanted to reach up to pat her hair. With a deep breath, her confidence returned.

"Come in," she invited, stepping back, feeling as if she had stepped into a new world where her life would never be the same. "Noah is still awake."

Two

As he entered a hallway his boot heels scraped on the polished oak floor. To his right through a wide-open archway, he glimpsed a piano in the corner of a large room with a hardwood floor and a brown leather sofa. To one side stood a large wooden desk. Marek drew a deep breath. An uncustomary nervousness plagued him, and he hoped he hid it. "I would like to see Noah," he answered in a voice that deepened and sounded strange to his ears.

She closed the door and motioned with a wave of her hand. "Come with me to the nursery. Both my sisters are here."

As he walked beside her, his pulse quickened while uncertainty grew with each step. "My nieces aren't babies any longer. I've forgotten how to deal with a baby. I don't remember much about them."

She laughed, a soft, delightful sound that made him relax slightly. "I'll admit, I had moments before he was born when

I felt terrified and overwhelmed. I've found out that you learn very fast when you have a baby to care for."

He placed a hand on her arm. "I'm sorry you were alone when he was born. I'm sorry Kern didn't live to be there. He would have been a huge support for you. I'll try to do what I think Kern would have wanted, but I can't take his place. Kern was unique."

"I hope you will, and it'll be wonderful if you do," she said.

He followed her into a playroom in shades of blue with paintings of animals hanging on the walls. Two other attractive women faced him. One was a pretty brunette in a red sweater and matching slacks, who stood looking at him with curious blue-green eyes. "Ashley, meet Marek Rangel, Noah's uncle. Marek, this is my sister Ashley Avanole." Camille turned slightly to another woman, who bore little resemblance to Camille or Ashley.

He was momentarily startled by the hostility in her cold gaze and assumed she didn't want him involved in Noah's life. "Stephanie, meet Marek Rangel. Marek, this is my sister Stephanie."

Marek greeted her, lost in thinking about being an uncle. His gaze shifted to the baby in a tire-shaped cushion on the floor.

Camille swept the baby up and held him, smiling and speaking softly to him. "Marek, meet your nephew, Noah Avanole." Noah waved his arms, blowing bubbles. She held him out to Marek, who took him carefully. He pulled the baby close, cradling him in his arms and looking down into twinkling, wide brown eyes that were filled with mischief as Noah blew bubbles and drooled. Marek felt weak-kneed as he had a moment of déjà vu. It was as if he were looking into Kern's eyes after he had played a joke on Marek. How could a little baby look like a grown man? If Marek had had a doubt before who had fathered this baby, it vanished now.

"He's Kern," he whispered without realizing he was speaking aloud. For a moment, he had a flash of the future, thinking this child and Ginny's girls would be the children in his life. Since the loss of Jillian, he never expected to marry or have a family. His arm tightened slightly around Noah. He felt a warmth toward the baby while they looked into each other's eyes; it was as if a tangible bond formed, which Marek knew was foolishness. From the first glance there was no way he could keep from loving this baby.

"He does seem to have a resemblance, but I'm going from memory and I thought maybe it was my imagination," Camille replied.

"There's more than a physical resemblance. He's like Kern. Is he always this happy?"

"Yes, he is," Camille answered, smiling and stepping closer to look at her son with Marek. "He's a wonderful baby."

Babbling unintelligible sounds, Noah blew more bubbles and Marek's smile broadened. "He's so tiny."

"He'll grow. He's gained weight and gotten much bigger since his birth." She gave him a moment longer. "If you're ready, I'll take him and we can go."

Marek handed Noah to her, brushing her arms and catching a whiff of an enticing jasmine scent. He hated to turn loose Noah, whose brown eyes gazed intently at him.

"And you're his nanny?" he asked Ashley, glancing at her and trying to politely include her.

"Yes. When he was born, I had to learn fast. Camille hired a nurse for the first month, so she taught me quite a bit. Being his nanny right now is a good job to have."

"And I help manage my sister's career," Stephanie interjected. "We love Noah very much."

Her tone was polite, but Marek's caution returned. Her glacial dark blue eyes held a warning, which reemphasized what he guessed was worry about his claims on Noah. For the first time, it occurred to Marek he might not ever have easy access to his nephew.

It was obvious the sisters were not in agreement about sharing Noah with his paternal relatives.

"It was nice to meet you," Ashley stated. Stephanie merely nodded perfunctorily, and Marek was certain about her feelings toward him. At the door he couldn't resist turning to glance back at Noah, who was playing with a rattle, kicking his legs and enjoying himself.

Marek's glance rested only briefly on Stephanie, who glared at him. Her mouth was set in a hard line. Marek followed Camille into the hall.

"I take it your sister Stephanie doesn't share your feelings about allowing Noah to know the paternal side of the family. I couldn't get a reading on what Ashley felt."

"Don't worry about Stephanie. Noah is my child, and I want you to know him. I told you, I want him to know the Rangels and ranching. I want you as an influence in his life. Ashley is all right with letting you see Noah."

"I'm glad," he said, "because we all want to know him. It's startling to me to look at him. There's something about him that really resembles Kern."

As they walked toward the front, he caught another whiff of the perfume she wore. When they passed the room with the piano, he glanced inside. "Is this where you practice your voice lessons?"

"Yes. It's an office of sorts, too. Stephanie wanted an office this spring to work on taxes. Noah disturbs her sometimes, so this room is the farthest from the nursery. I study languages every day, trying to improve my grasp of Italian, French and German. Wherever we go, I take my own furniture, so that's why we have such a minimal amount. I like having my own bed. But I rent the piano. I can't practice in a hotel."

"Good idea. I don't blame you. It sounds like it works out well," Marek said, thinking she must not have much time in her life for Noah.

In minutes they were in his black limousine, headed toward the airport. He sat facing her. "I feel as if my life is changing and I don't have control over the changes," he said. "That's unusual. I'd like to work out something before you leave Texas. Something that's permanent as far as seeing him periodically," he added. He'd like to see more of her. She interested him and seemed different from other women he had known.

"We may have to have those lawyers yet," she replied.

"Let's try to work it out between us," he urged, thinking she had a flair for the dramatic in her manner and her dress. Once again, she stood out with her midnight hair secured with a blue scarf and her deep blue dress that emphasized her lush curves and narrow waist. Her startling pale blue eyes were a vivid contrast to her thick, black lashes.

He had never associated with women in show business, much less in opera. She was an unknown in many ways. His gaze rested on her full, enticing lips. What would it be like to kiss her? His question startled him. He hadn't noticed any women in a personal way since losing Jillian, but Camille was bringing him back into the world without any effort to do so. She had been forthright, businesslike about Noah. Yet his physical response to her was becoming more personal. "I have a lot of resources. I have a plane available at all times. Most of the time I can come and go as I please. We should be able to adjust schedules," he said.

"We'll try. I might be out of the United States some of the time."

"Let's take it as it comes," he suggested, wondering whether they could ever work out an acceptable plan for sharing Noah. "Tell me about your life," he said, his curiosity about her growing. "I'm sorry I don't already know about you, but I haven't been into opera."

She smiled at him. "Then I believe you are in for a treat, but that's because I love it. You will either love it or not care for it at all. To me it's the most beautiful music possible."

Her enthusiasm made him smile. "So you've always dreamed of this career?"

"Yes, actually. I started singing early and began voice lessons when I was young. Now, looking back, it seems like forever."

He listened while she talked about growing up in Saint Louis and singing, and he wondered about her past. When she paused in her talk, he leaned closer.

"Have you ever been in love?"

"Not really. I thought I was in college, but it was never that serious. I really haven't had much time for a social life since."

"Maybe you should take some time."

She laughed. "With a baby now? I don't think this is the time. There's no room for romance in my life. A baby plus an opera career—those would send anyone running."

"Maybe running with you, but not from you—take another look in your mirror."

"Thank you," she said, smiling at him. "Seriously, I haven't given a lot of thought to what I'll do in the future. I need to start looking into schools for Noah."

Marek smiled. "You have time."

"It flies past, and I may pick a school where he has to go on a waiting list."

Marek's thoughts shifted to Noah. He had to think of a way to keep the baby in the family. He couldn't sit by while she went to France or Germany or Italy for a year and took Noah with her.

He took Camille to a quiet, elegant dinner club in Houston. The decor was dark blue, with dark walnut paneling and dimmed crystal chandeliers. It was a place he had gone often, and he felt they would not be disturbed by fans or his friends, but he had forgotten about the dancing. There was a small dance floor; out of courtesy he felt he needed to ask her to dance. He remembered holding Jillian in his arms, laughing at something she had said. He didn't want to dance with this woman who was so alive and who made him feel so alive.

He realized he had ceased talking during dinner.

"You're thinking about your fiancée," Camille remarked. "Again, I'm sorry for your loss. It's understandable for you to think about her. My guess is that you both came here to eat occasionally."

"You're right. Sorry if I got distracted. That's past, but there are moments it comes rushing back. Would you like to dance?"

"You don't have to dance," she said, smiling. "This is fine."

Relieved, appreciating her understanding, he wanted to accept her reply and forget dancing, but he had to pick up the pieces and go on with life. He stood. "C'mon. It'll do me good to get out there and move around."

It was the first time he had danced since he had been with Jillian. He took a deep breath and focused on Camille, smiling at her.

"You really don't have to dance if you'd rather not," she said gently, startling him.

"It shows that much?" he asked, focusing on her more intently.

"Maybe a little. I can also imagine," she added gently.

"Do you like to dance?" he asked, leading her to the dance floor.

"Yes, but if you want to stop, I'll understand why."

He took her lightly into his arms. "You're sensitive to other people," he said, studying her large, thickly lashed eyes. "You look beautiful tonight," he added, and she smiled.

"Thank you."

"I mean it." As he danced the first few steps, he had another moment when pain stabbed him. He missed Jillian, her slender body, her laughter. He focused on Camille and the moment passed. "I just know how I would feel if I were in your position."

"You never saw Kern any other time?"

"No. The weekend I met your brother was the only time I was with him. While I had a wonderful time with him, we really weren't that close."

"Kern was the embodiment of charm and fun." He realized she was as easy to dance with as she was to talk to. Her perfume was enticing, and the low vee of her neckline revealed the beginning of full, soft curves.

"Do you want a bigger family—a husband, maybe a sibling for Noah?"

"Yes, at some distant future point in my life. But right now I have a career to pursue, and it's on the rise. I have a baby to take care of and he's most important."

A fast number began, and, in seconds, he was dancing with enthusiasm. It felt good to move, and he liked to watch her. She was an energetic, sensual dancer. While he moved, cares and heartaches dropped away and burdens lifted from his shoulders.

A samba followed and they continued dancing. He shrugged off his suit jacket and draped it over an empty chair at the edge of the dance floor. He looked at Camille's mass of black hair and wished she had left it loose. She was enticing, melting away some of his hurt and numbness. As the dance ended, he pulled her close to lean over in a dip.

When he gazed into her blue eyes, desire stirred, feelings that had ceased after his loss. Startled he swung Camille up, smiling at her.

The realization that he was beginning to get over his loss shocked him.

When a slow ballad started, he drew Camille into his arms to dance. "I have to admit, the dancing is fun. I haven't done this in a while. Maybe it's therapeutic."

"Actually, it probably is," she said. "Dancing is definitely good for me. It's relaxing, and you're extremely good at it."

"Thanks. You've made it easy for me," he said. Once again, he had a flash of awareness of her. He held her in his arms, and they gazed into each other's eyes. The moment changed, became personal. Feelings that had been dormant in him for over a year stirred again, stronger this time. He looked at her full, sensuous, curving lips.

The number ended, and they returned to the linen-covered table. By the time he sat facing her, his thoughts were partially on the baby again.

"Do you know your schedule for the rest of the year?"

"Yes. After Dallas, Santa Fe and Saint Louis, I leave for Budapest in October, and I will be there until December. Next March I will be in New York at the Met, where I'm not the lead but thrilled to perform."

"Budapest, New York—hell of a long way from Texas."

"I'm sorry, but that's my life at this point."

"I understand. We'll work on it as long as you want us to be part of his life. In the meantime, can we arrange a meeting where my sister can see Noah?"

Before Camille could answer, white china plates with greens were placed in front of them. When they were alone again, Camille set down her water goblet. "I'm sure we can work out a time for your sister to see Noah. Actually, the weekend is coming up. Saturday morning would be a good time for us. Mornings are better because Noah will be awake. He'll nap in the afternoon. I'll have my voice practice, and I schedule time regularly for exercise, but I won't stay with you anyway, so that won't matter."

"I'll let you know about Saturday morning. I need to run that past my sister because she has a family. I'd like to bring someone else with me, if I may. My ranch foreman has been with us all my life. He's like a member of the family to me, and he was to Kern. I'd like him to see Noah."

"Of course," she said, smiling warmly. "You're not exactly like I thought you'd be," she added, studying him. "You're not like Kern, either."

"Definitely not like Kern," he said. "So what did you expect?" Marek asked, amused and curious. When her cheeks turned pink, his curiosity grew. "You're blushing. Your opinion must have been not so great. Now I'm curious."

"You're more friendly than I thought you'd be," she said, her cheeks growing even more red. "I thought you would be like you were the first few minutes at your office."

He smiled. "I'll have to improve my image. I'll have to admit, I wasn't friendly at my office. I thought you wanted a donation for something to do with the opera."

She laughed, a light, inviting sound, making him want to cause her to laugh often.

Conversation shifted to other topics. For the next hour over dinner, he enjoyed her company and enjoyed being out for the evening with a beautiful woman again.

Later, when they returned to the dance floor, he found it was easier. He still thought of Jillian, still missed her badly, but he had better control of his emotions and he was happier about dancing. "I really would like to see Noah again before

Saturday. Is there anytime that would be convenient for me to drop by when he's awake?"

"Of course. Just call ahead. Come tomorrow when you want. I'll be home. I have a voice lesson, a workout and a French lesson, but I can break away briefly. We'll be happy to see you."

"When do you have free time?"

"I have some to be with Noah. There are moments my life is like everyone else's. We're all busy."

"Very well. I'll come in the morning if that's all right."

"It's fine. It might give Ashley a bit of a break. Stephanie will vanish with errands, so you won't cross paths with her."

"She feels that strongly about me," he said, shaking his head.

"She's just scared."

"She doesn't need to be afraid I'm taking your baby. I would never do that. No judge would let me anyway."

"Oh, one might. I think you have a lot of influence in this state."

"How I wish. Where was Noah born?"

"Oddly enough, I had a special performance here and he was born in Texas. I had excellent care. I was in a Dallas hospital."

Marek smiled. "So we have another Rangel who's a Texan. That would please Kern."

"I think it pleases you."

"Yes, it does," he said.

"I don't think I've mentioned it, but I named him Noah Kern Avanole. I hope you don't object."

"I'm glad you did. Did you tell Kern what you planned to name him?"

"Of course, and he was delighted."

"I'll bet he was. I'm still amazed he didn't call me. Usually Kern didn't keep things to himself. Noah Kern Avanole. Good name."

"Thank you. I thought so. Right now is a good time for everyone to see him. When I'm performing, I won't be as free."

"That's what I figured," Marek said, thinking she had a face and figure to have gone into movies instead of opera. They danced until she mentioned the time and said she had to get home.

They talked all the way during the flight back to Dallas and by the time he brought her to her condo door, he realized he had enjoyed the evening. Impulsively, he took her hand.

"I've enjoyed getting to know you. I still can't tell you how much I appreciate you sharing Noah with us. There aren't words for that."

"I'm glad you're happy about him and interested in him."

"I hope your sister stops worrying. I'll never try to take Noah from you."

"Stephanie will be all right. She's just scared right now because you can do more for him than we can. I don't think she understands how I feel as a mother, wanting him to know his father's family, to know ranching. That's important to me."

"I'm glad," he said lightly, leaning forward to brush a kiss on her cheek, catching the scent of her perfume again. Her skin was soft and smooth, and he was grateful to her for making the evening enjoyable. "I'll see you in the morning. I'll call before I come by."

"Fine," she said, smiling at him. She stepped inside and closed the door.

On the drive to the ranch, he had time to consider the evening. The vision of Camille dancing around him remained indelibly etched in memory. He thought about Noah and holding him in his arms. Camille would be in Santa Fe this summer, Budapest in the fall. How could he keep Noah in their lives in Texas when he would be far away with his mother? Noah was too tiny now to take him away from her for a long visit.

Saturday morning Camille showered and dressed in blue slacks and a matching shirt. As she pinned up her hair, Ashley stood watching her. "You've gone out with him three nights this week, and he's been here to see Noah every day. He's crazy about Noah."

"He'll be a good father figure for Noah," Camille remarked.

"I'm beginning to wonder whether Steph is right. Is Marek going to want to have custody of Noah? Or is there any chance part of it is he's coming to see you, too?"

Camille laughed. "No. He's interested in Noah." Her smile faded. "He's still having difficulty about losing his fiancée, although he seemed to get a grip on those feelings when we were dancing." She pulled a brush through more long strands of hair before pinning them up. "As far as Noah is concerned, Marek has told me repeatedly that he won't ever try to take Noah from me. I know he wants to be part of Noah's life, and I think he should be. I want Noah to be part of the Rangel family. He needs to know them. Marek can show him a cowboy's life."

"Some cowboy," Ashley said, laughing. "He's a billionaire."

"Ashley, he's a good guy. He truly likes the baby, and he's promised me he won't try to take him. We'll work out something everyone can live with."

"Let me have Noah before you have to change again," Ashley said, taking Noah from Camille. He went willingly, happy to be carried. Camille brushed a kiss on his cheek.

"I won't let anyone take him from us," Camille said quietly, feeling fairly certain Marek meant what he said. What little Kern had said about his brother indicated that he was a man of his word, yet that might have been the man Kern knew.

Thursday when Marek had come to see his nephew, she had watched him hold the baby and talk to him. All the hesitation and uncertainty Marek had shown that first time he had held Noah had disappeared. She left them alone for a time, and, when she returned, Marek was seated on the floor, holding Noah and talking to him about a large, brightly colored ball and rolling it around for him.

Marek had glanced at her and smiled, his attention quickly returning to Noah. She was constantly reminded of Marek's loss because he seemed cool and distant in many ways. She suspected he rarely saw her as anything more than Noah's mom, which, under the circumstances, was just as well.

"Camille, you haven't heard a word I've said to you," Ashley said as she finished changing Noah.

"Sorry, Ash, I was lost in thought about Marek."

"I can see why. He's a good-looking man. Even more so than his brother. I never really saw his brother in person, just pictures, so maybe that's not fair."

"He's more handsome, but he has none of the laid-back charm his younger brother did. He's far more serious."

"You each have serious issues to deal with—how Noah will be raised, plus the personal issues. Can you trust Marek and will he ever get over his loss? Maybe he's charming when there's nothing at stake."

"You're probably right. His fiancée was stunning, constantly in society pages, and I'm sure photographers loved to take her picture. No woman can be as beautiful as she was."

"I have to agree with you. Her pictures look like she was a movie star or top model."

"He's still grieving for her, but now Noah is a distraction from his loss."

"The crash was dreadful. His grief is understandable. I'll

have Noah ready when they come. I want to get him fed now before I try to clean him up or dress him."

"I can feed him," Camille said, reaching for her baby.

"Not if you don't want to have to change again. You're dressed and ready. Let me run the risk of him blowing breakfast or spitting up."

Laughing, Camille shrugged. "He's yours. I'm nervous about meeting Marek's sister."

"Why on earth would you be nervous?"

Camille shrugged. "I suppose since she's the mother of two. I feel like she knows more about babies. I'm still a novice at this."

"Don't be ridiculous. Besides, Marek is nice. A little fierce-looking sometimes. And a heartbreaker. I pity anyone who falls in love with him. Since he's still grieving over his fiancée and brother, he isn't going to want to lose Noah, too. I still think Steph may be right on this one."

"Time will tell, but I don't think so," Camille replied, feeling a tiny knot of worry surface. In spite of his reassurances and his brother's good opinion of him, the nagging fear wouldn't go away.

Two hours later, after introductions had been made and she and Marek had talked briefly, she gathered her sisters and left Marek and his sister and foreman with Noah.

At the end of their visit with Noah, Marek flew back to the ranch with Jess and worked beside him the rest of the day, finding release for pent-up feelings in sheer physical labor. He did the same on Sunday, mulling over his options regarding Noah. Sunday evening he saw Jess in the corral riding a new horse.

Marek grabbed his Stetson and went out, stretching out his legs as he walked to the corral. He perched on the fence to watch Jess work with the quarter horse. Jess turned, riding close and swinging down out of the saddle. "This is a fine horse."

"You've got him as gentle as a lamb."

"That's what I mean. He's a good one. You made an excellent purchase. Want to ride him for a minute?"

"Sure," Marek replied, jumping down from the fence and climbing into the saddle. He circled the corral, urging the horse to a trot. When he finished, he returned to Jess to dismount.

"Here he is, as good as you said." He handed the reins to Jess and walked beside him as he led the horse into the stable. In the cool shadows Marek leaned against a post to watch Jess unsaddle the horse.

"I've been thinking what I can do about little Noah. Whatever we do, we can't take him from Camille. Her sisters are crazy about him, too. I don't want to hurt anyone, but we have to be part of his life and be able to watch him grow. He's a tie to Kern that I want in our lives."

"I can't see any simple solution, but I'm not thinking on it too much because that's your worry," Jess said, lifting the saddle off the horse.

"It's worrying Ginny, and I can't sleep nights for trying to come up with a workable answer. I can't imagine Camille letting me have Noah for any significant amount of time."

"I agree with you."

"Ginny reminded me of how take-charge she thinks I am and how she thinks I've spent my life getting everyone to do what I want. I don't quite see it that way, but she's told me this time I won't be able to do that."

"Sometimes we just have to adjust to what life hands us."

"Jess, I don't go into things expecting to fail. I've looked at this every way I can think of. There's no easy answer, but I may have something workable if I can persuade Camille to cooperate."

"All you can do is try. And if she says no, try something else," Jess stated shortly, beginning to groom the sorrel.

"I don't think you'll like it."

"All right. Tell me. How do you plan to get her to agree?" Jess asked, frowning slightly as he studied Marek.

The following Friday night, a spring evening with the sun slanting in the sky, Camille sat across from Marek. They were on his patio at his Dallas home. Steaks had just been put on the grill. She was sipping her glass of wine while Marek had a barely touched martini. She had dressed with care in a red cotton sundress with high-heeled sandals and her hair was up on her head. She suspected she could have worn a gunnysack and Marek would not have noticed. She still didn't think he ever saw her as a woman, which was just as well because she didn't want to get into a relationship with any man at this point in her life.

Tonight, it seemed he was taking his time because he had not brought up the subject of what arrangements he hoped to make with her regarding Noah, which he had said was the purpose of asking her to dinner. She had no intention of rushing him, either. She had mulled it over constantly and the most workable plan she and Ashley could devise was for her to always get a home large enough for the Rangels to come visit when they wanted. They would be welcome wherever she lived, either here or abroad. If she could get a wing where they could stay off to themselves, she thought they might be happier. She couldn't imagine leaving Noah behind in Texas. She and Ashley had agreed on that one and she had constantly reassured Stephanie she would stick to that decision.

Taking a deep breath, Camille hoped to calm her nerves. A steady uneasiness plagued her because she had big doubts that he would agree to what she intended to offer.

She watched him stand over the steaks, which were sending a spiral of gray smoke into the air. When he had arrived at her house to pick her up in a limousine, he had looked as commanding and successful as ever. Wearing a charcoal suit and red tie, he looked ready for an evening out. Had the suit been meant to be a reminder of his wealth and power? Enticing smells of the grilling meat would usually tempt her, but her stomach churned. Marek seemed strong willed, a man totally accustomed to getting his way. His fortune held a possible threat like a twister spinning on her horizon.

Marek picked up his drink and returned to sit near her. "Steaks will be done soon. I hope you have an appetite."

"I'll admit I'm nervous, and that's killing my appetite. I'm far more anxious over this than going onstage."

"Don't be disturbed," he said quietly. "We'll work something out, hopefully to the satisfaction of all and in Noah's best interests as well. He can't participate in this, but he has the biggest stake."

"That's true," she said, feeling better that Marek sounded as if he would put Noah first.

Marek leaned forward to take her hand lightly in his. His compelling dark eyes made her breath catch. Why was she having this reaction to him?

"Relax, Camille," he said in a gentle tone. "We'll try to find a solution that will be in *everyone's* best interest."

"I hope so. That's what I've prayed for," she replied, aware of the jump in her pulse. She was certain it was a very one-sided attraction that she shouldn't have to him. And she couldn't guess what he was going to ask her to do regarding Noah.

"Relax, have some wine, eat some steak. Let's have dinner and then we'll talk about Noah."

She nodded, unable to speak. Smiling, he patted her hand

and sat back to raise his drink. "Here's to a happy solution and to you and Kern having a beautiful, adorable son."

She had to return his smile as she touched his glass lightly. "I'll have to drink to that," she said, taking a tiny sip.

"And I have to say, my brother always had great taste in his female friends," he added with an uncustomary smile as he raised his glass to her.

It was the closest he had come to flirting. "Thank you. I'm not sure about great taste. Perhaps we were thrown together on a festive occasion and everything clicked."

"You have a great little boy. Thank you for letting me know about him."

"I've told you why. I'm pleased that you're responding in a positive way."

He smiled and sipped his drink before glancing at the cooker. "I'll get the steaks."

They ate outside at a glass-topped table with dinner served by his staff. After dinner they moved back to the lawn chairs overlooking the pool and yard. The staff quietly cleared the table, and, when they were left alone, Marek turned his chair to face her.

"Tell me what you propose," he said. He listened as she talked about getting a place wherever she went that would be large enough for all of them and how he and his family could visit whenever and however long they chose.

Marek simply listened and nodded, and her heart raced as she talked. Her palms had grown damp.

After she finished, he sat quietly, sipping a tall glass of iced tea. She waited in silence, letting him take his time. It seemed eons before he set down his drink and spoke.

"That's a feasible plan," he said, and she let out her breath. She couldn't relax completely because she was certain he had something else in mind.

"I have another idea. All I ask is for you to listen to what

I propose. Don't give me an answer tonight—we can talk about it. I want you to think it over before you answer."

"That sounds reasonable but scary."

He smiled again, a smile that softened his features and made him slightly less intimidating. "Good. You are totally tied up in your career and Noah, right?"

"Yes. You know that."

"I lost my fiancée, and I'm not interested in a deep commitment. Jillian had my heart. I enjoy women and the day will come when I won't be so numb with grief, but I can't imagine ever loving again. What I'm getting at is both of us have set loving one special person on hold, more or less."

"You're right," she said, her curiosity soaring.

"Camille, will you marry me? A marriage of convenience would help both of us and should be so much better for Noah."

Stunned, she dropped her glass of tea, barely aware of it shattering on the patio.

Three

"Please don't answer me now because I want you to think about it. Any answer you give me immediately will be a knee-jerk reaction. Marry me—it'll be a marriage of convenience in the fullest sense," he repeated. "At some point I would expect us to have a physical relationship. I think it would be unrealistic to expect otherwise."

His voice sounded as if it came from far away, and she felt light-headed. Marry him! "Sorry, I think I'm going to faint."

He stopped talking instantly and stood. "Put your head down for a moment." She did as he said and soon felt a cold wet cloth being placed gently on the back of her neck. His warm fingers on her nape were disturbing in a far different way than his proposal had been.

As her head cleared, she sat up.

"Take a deep breath or two and just relax."

"I broke your glass," she said, glancing at the sparkling shards at her feet.

"Forget that. Just relax a moment. The proposal is a surprise, and that's why I want you to think about it. When you feel clear and are ready to hear them, I can give you reasons I came up with this solution."

"I suppose I'm ready."

He studied her, and she gazed back, trying to calm down enough to listen to him. She wanted to blurt out a refusal now. Why would she have to think it over? How could he have ever expected her to accept?

"Marriage will give Noah the Rangel name. If we're married, I think you'll feel better about leaving him with me. We'll work out times you can live with. I'll be a dad for him. I would like to adopt him."

"I'll lose him," she whispered. "He'll be your son in every way except one. You'll have far more claim over him than you will as his uncle."

"You won't lose him—I promise. And we will have a prenuptial agreement, a contract that you will approve. I will work with you on when I can be with him. I will see to it that financially you and Noah are completely taken care of. You'll have a private plane whenever you want. You'll have a generous allowance. You'll be more financially free to pursue your career. I know you're doing well, but I can help you do better, and I can definitely do a lot for Noah."

"I don't need money."

"I know you don't, but this will make it easier. Definitely better for him."

"I want to do well with my career."

"I expect you to," he said. He took her hand again. While his hand held hers, his thumb brushed her knuckles lightly, keeping her aware of his contact. *Married to him.* Even as the proposal seemed impossible, the prospect made her pulse race.

"I hope to be part of Noah's life," Marek continued. "I

want to be an influence in his life, to get to know him. By proposing, I feel I'm doing what Kern would have done if it had been my baby. I loved my brother. I just want to watch Noah grow up. I feel as if it gives me a tie to Kern," Marek said, his voice deepening.

Camille's eyes filled with tears.

"Camille," he said quietly. "I don't want to hurt or worry you. I want you to be happy with whatever we do."

"How can I be happy with this? You'll have Noah, and I won't be able to do anything about it?" she cried, standing and walking away in embarrassment that she couldn't control her tears.

He came up behind her to place his hands on her shoulders and turn her to face him. He framed her face with his hands and wiped away her tears with his thumbs.

"Stop crying. I promised I wouldn't hurt you," he said gently. "Causing you distress is not what I intended. If I were Kern and had just proposed—the two of you were not in love—wouldn't you consider his proposal?"

Startled by his question, she gazed up at Marek while silence stretched. What would he do if she refused to marry him? He was far more powerful and had more resources. "I suppose I would give it thought," she replied.

"I'm not Kern, but, believe me, I have his interests at heart."

Mulling over what he said, she decided she would have given some serious thought to a proposal if it had been from Kern. "You're a little more serious and forceful than Kern."

Marek's faint smile lifted one corner of his mouth, calming her slightly. "I'll try to be less 'forceful.' All I ask is for you to think about the possibilities. Now, are you ready to hear what I propose in the way of finances?"

"Another surprise," she said without thinking. "Finances are really incidental. That's not the issue here."

He released her. "I know it's not the issue, but I think we ought to look at all aspects of this. Finances, arrangements, a physical relationship. Want some more tea while we talk?"

His voice deepened, and that surprising fire he could ignite effortlessly between them sent a shiver to her toes. With the flicker in the depth of his dark eyes, she guessed he felt the same sparks, too. "Yes, thank you," she said, walking to the outdoor kitchen with him and watching while he poured another tall glass of tea for her. This handsome, wealthy Texas rancher intended to marry her. The idea was impossible.

After retrieving his tea, he directed her to a chair away from the broken glass and slid his chair close to hers.

As she sipped the icy tea, she focused on him. His eyes gave away nothing about his feelings. He could have been discussing the weather as far as his demeanor and expression were concerned.

"We will draw up papers so our arrangements are as binding as any contract. If you accept, I will pay you five million dollars."

Her shock returned full force. What were his real intentions? To offer that much money, was he working toward getting custody of Noah? "If I marry you, I get five million dollars from you," she repeated.

"That's right," he said quietly. "You'll get one million when we sign the papers and four million as soon as we are husband and wife. You will get a million each year we are married, plus a generous allowance. I will set up a trust for Noah and pay for everything for him. You can spend the money I give you as you please because there will be no strings."

Her shock mushroomed over the fortune that he was dangling as an inducement to accept what he wanted. She could only stare at him, speechless over his offer that would transform her life and the lives of every member of her family. The money was both frightening and dazzling. "Now I see why you get your way so often," she whispered without even realizing she had spoken aloud.

She had been counting on her career to help her family. With this money she wouldn't have to worry whether she made stardom or not. Life should be far easier, and yet…

"That's a huge amount of money," she said, thinking it was an even bigger power play. Marek looked relaxed, as if accustomed to bargaining with such high stakes, but these were the highest possible as far as she was concerned. This cool rancher had thought this out and come up with an offer that she might be unable to refuse.

"I can afford it and I'd want to do it. If you say yes, you'll be giving me far more because I know I will become a permanent part of Noah's life."

"You hardly know Noah. How can you feel this strongly about him?"

"It's easy," Marek replied. "I feel this strongly about my brother. This baby is a definite tie to Kern."

She nodded, touched and aware how vulnerable he was where his heart was concerned. "I can understand that." She rubbed her forehead. "Wow. You've turned my life topsy-turvy. Actually, if I accept your offer—my whole family will be topsy-turvy. That fortune will change all our lives. You'll want Noah a lot of the time. I'm sure you've thought about how much."

"You and I would live in the same place some of the time. I don't want to give up being a rancher or living on my ranch. But I don't do that all the time now, and I can give up some of the time. When Noah gets to school age, you'll have to give serious thought to how much he will travel with you."

"I know, but I can't foresee what my career will be. It's filled with uncertainties at this point."

"You'll have enough money that you can give it up completely if you want."

Momentarily, her tension lightened, and she smiled. "No, I've dreamed of this all my life, and things are beginning to open up for me. At this point, I definitely do not want to toss aside what I've gained. I want to sing. I want to be a star. I love opera. But I love Noah and I want what's best for him."

"Then I think you'll have to seriously consider my offer."

"I suppose I will," she said, gazing beyond him, watching the splashing water in the fountain in the pool. "This is a beautiful place."

"This is my Dallas home. The best place is the ranch."

"I know very little about ranches."

He reached over again to take her hand. "Camille, Kern was drawn to you, and I feel certain he would have proposed. I think you and I can have a workable arrangement that will benefit Noah. I've tried to do what will benefit you. This million a year I've offered—your monthly allowance will be enough that you shouldn't need to touch that money. You should be able to invest it and I can help you and make it grow. I want what will make you happy—as happy as I will be if you accept."

"Suppose you fall in love with someone later?"

"Divorce still exists, but I don't expect to fall in love again in my life. I gave my heart to Jillian." He looked away, and she instantly regretted bringing up a subject that would open his wounds.

This time she reached out to touch his arm, placing her hand on him. "Marek, I didn't mean to cause you hurt."

He inhaled deeply. "Sometimes it just comes out of the blue, and I feel weak in the knees. Don't apologize. You had no way of knowing."

"You talked about a physical relationship. I won't have a lot of time, and I'm not about to jump into one when we're strangers," she said. "I did that once in my life, and I won't do it again. Your brother charmed and captivated me that night. Now, a physical relationship will have to come later, maybe much later."

"I keep busy at the ranch and try to do the hard, physical jobs. That's helped. Remember, we'll be married. You're a beautiful woman, Camille. You're getting shortchanged here, but you've told me you don't have time for a man in your life and I won't be in the way or demand your time. A physical relationship will have to be mutual."

His answer reassured her. She smiled. "You'll probably hope I'll disappear for months on end."

One corner of his mouth lifted in a crooked grin that she realized was about the best he would do for a smile most of the time. "I won't be hoping any such thing," he said. "We can work out a schedule. You think about what you'd like for a schedule."

"I can't even imagine. What about when I'm in New Mexico this summer?"

"You decide what you want, and I'll look at it and we'll go from there."

She thought about all he had said to her as they sat in silence. "How different this might have been if Kern had lived," she remarked, going from memories about Kern to thinking the two brothers were so different in looks, personalities, in nearly every way. The only similarity was their blood tie and their shared love of ranching.

"I still think he would have proposed and done something to convince you to marry him. He wouldn't have wanted to leave Texas, either, any more than I do."

She studied Marek's handsome features. Mrs. Marek Rangel. The idea took her breath away and seemed totally impossible. Millions would be hers. She thought of all the things she could do for Noah and for her family. Marek would do so much for Noah that she wouldn't have to factor in what she could do. It was staggering to try to deal with his proposal. But this was about so much more than money. It would give her a father figure for Noah. It would make him close with the Rangel family, and he would know ranching and a cowboy's life. These were all things she wanted and the reason she had contacted Marek in the first place.

She had to think about his offer, discuss it with her sisters and with her family. Silence stretched between them. He sat watching the fountain, sipping his iced tea. How much had his solitary life contributed to this proposal? To lose his brother and his fiancée—the two people he was closest to and loved—that would be devastating for anyone. She could see why he had latched on to Noah so swiftly.

She studied his profile, his full black hair and thickly lashed eyes. What if she married him and fell in love with him? She didn't want that distraction to her career. Even worse, Marek wouldn't return her love, and that would be devastating. There were no doubts he would be agreeable to a physical relationship, but anything more? She believed what he said, that he would never love again. The pictures of Jillian had been breathtakingly beautiful.

"I guess I should go home and think about this. We've discussed it tonight, and I'm at least getting adjusted to thinking about your offer."

"Good," he said, giving her a bigger smile. "You'll have to give up Noah sometimes, but you'll be busy. You would have to anyway because of your career."

She nodded and stood. "I think I really should go."

He stood to take her arm. His slight touch caused another jump in her pulse. "I'll see you home. Take as long as you need to consider my proposal and to talk to your family about it. When would you like to go out again?"

"Tomorrow I want to be with family. This is Friday. I'd

prefer to wait until Tuesday to see you," she said, thinking this would also give her time to talk to her attorney. "This will send my sisters into orbit. If I accept your proposal, our lives will have major changes."

"Not anything you can't live with, I hope. I tried to find something that would benefit all of us."

Marek climbed into the limousine with her. As the limo pulled away, her gaze roamed over the colonial house with massive Corinthian columns along the front porch. This would be her home, too, if she married him. Dazed, she couldn't envision that ever happening.

"Your parents will be all right with our marriage if I accept?" she asked as the limo drove through the tall iron gates.

"I'm a grown man. Yes, I expect them to be all right with it. They've made a life for themselves in California and are busy all the time with social and charitable activities. Dad plays golf and recently fell and broke his ankle, so he's on crutches right now, which will slow him down about traveling to Texas. My mom hates to fly and they usually drive, but that's out until Dad's ankle heals."

"I'm sorry about that."

"You'll definitely pass inspection. Although they loved Jillian. They were heartbroken over the crash besides being so hurt over the loss of Kern."

"That's understandable."

"I've thought this proposal over. You're beautiful, and you're a rising opera star. They sounded impressed."

"This is their first grandson. Is that correct? Your sister has two girls."

"That's right. My parents are not into grandchildren as much as a lot of parents or they wouldn't live over a thousand miles away."

"So your sister is the person you'll be concerned about. I assume she's happy with this."

"She doesn't know about it yet. I wanted to talk to you first."

"Have you told Mr. Grayson?"

"Yes, I discussed it with him. Jess approves."

"That surprises me. You're very close to him, aren't you?"

"Sometimes I think he's more my dad than my own father. He taught me a lot about the ranch. He's been around as far back as I can remember. I'm closer to him than I am to my parents. They were always busy, but Jess had time for me and Kern. Actually, for Ginny, too, but she didn't hang out with him when she became a teenager. I did a lot. Now Jess is a best friend, maybe sometimes still a dad."

"You can't beat that combination," she said, smiling at him. "I'm glad you have someone like that even though no one can take away your grief or replace your brother. But your sister may not be happy to see you marry without love."

"Ginny will adjust. She knows I'm doing what I want. I take it you're close to your sisters."

"I'm closest to Ashley," Camille replied. She lapsed into silence for a time. "My head is spinning with all this. I can't believe this is happening."

"My offer is real, and I hope you accept. I know you didn't have it in your plans to share Noah a lot of the time, but I think when we do this, it will work out where both of us are happy. I hope you'd rather have him with Jess and me out on the ranch some of the time than backstage going from pillar to post."

"Backstage is exciting to me, but backstage will not begin to hold the draw for him that your ranch will."

"If you accept, the Circle R will be his ranch, too," Marek replied. Startled, she stared at him, thinking about all the changes in their lives. If she married Marek, Noah would become Marek's heir.

She shook her head. "The whole thing is staggering.

You're a very wealthy, powerful man. I forget about that when I'm with you, but then moments come when I'm reminded about your status. Is this a command instead of an offer?"

"Of course not. We'll negotiate, but I've tried to be generous."

"You've been generous far beyond my imagination. When I met Kern, I didn't know how wealthy your family is. I'm not from Texas and at that time had never heard of the Rangels. Your brother was so down-to-earth and unpretentious. He was filled with fun and he was sort of happy-go-lucky. I didn't dream he had this fortune. I didn't know that until after the weekend."

"That was Kern absolutely. Money meant little to him. We were born into wealth, and I've increased it. Kern worked for me and he helped. I've been lucky, but after a point where you're comfortable and fed and have necessities, the wealth is not what makes you happy."

"Whatever it was, your brother was a happy man."

"If Kern had lived, you would have been Mrs. Kern Rangel. He would have charmed you into accepting. Kern wouldn't have given up."

They both became silent for the rest of the ride. At her door he took her hands. "Listen to me. Don't worry. I want you to be happy. You're Noah's mother, and Kern would have done anything he could to make you happy. The last thing I want to do is hurt you. We'll work out something here. This is a start, but I thought a marriage, even though it is definitely a marriage of convenience, would be the best solution for all. Especially for Noah."

She nodded, aware of him standing close, holding her hands, trying his best to be nice to her while trying to persuade her to accept his offer. If they married, could she avoid losing her heart to him? Or letting the marriage destroy her career?

"I'm a little overwhelmed. Actually, a lot overwhelmed. I'll talk to my sisters and my family and try to get accustomed to the idea. Start thinking about a few more details regarding when Noah would be with you and when he would be with me," she said, realizing before the words were out of her mouth that he had probably already planned what they would do.

"You tell me what you want on that," he said, surprising her.

"He's too little to leave with you."

"One more thing to think about—when I have him, will Ashley stay? I'll need a nanny."

Startled, Camille stared at him. "I hadn't thought about that, but she would stay with Noah. I'd want her to continue as his nanny. I'll have to ask because she may not want to do so. Staying on your Texas ranch would be entirely different for her than traveling with both of her sisters."

"That's right. But if she'll do it, I'd prefer her to remain his nanny. I think everyone will be happier, including Noah."

"If she stays, it'll completely change her life."

He gave that faint crooked smile again. "I hope it's not that big a change. We have a great ranch and I'm usually working from sunup to sundown, so I won't be underfoot. I'll pay her salary. Whatever it is, you can promise her a raise."

"You're generous."

"If you let me have Noah part of the time, you'll be the most generous."

Once again he framed her face with his hands. "Camille, I'll try my best to make you happy. I just want to be part of his life and so does Ginny."

"I understand. I want you to be in his life. That's why I contacted you in the first place."

She gazed into his earnest dark eyes and wondered about their future. She had tied her life to his and there was no turning back now. He was unbelievably handsome, and her heart drummed. He leaned forward to brush a light kiss on her forehead, and then he stepped away. "I'll call you about Tuesday."

He turned and headed to his limo in long strides.

Dazed, Camille stepped inside, locked the door and leaned against it. Ashley stood waiting farther down the darkened hallway.

"I didn't think you were ever coming inside. I know you weren't smooching out there, so what was going on?"

"I have to talk to you. I assume Noah is asleep. Where is Stephanie?"

"Stephanie is out with the latest guy. Noah is asleep. You're later than I thought you'd be. We can go anywhere to talk. The baby monitors are on."

"Let's go to my room. Let me see Noah for just a second. I promise I won't wake him."

"Sure. What did you do tonight?" Ashley asked.

"We went to his Dallas home and he cooked steaks. He had a staff to do everything else."

"I can't even imagine. What's the home like?"

"Not as fancy and elegant as I expected. Upper scale, nice, but not knock-your-socks-off elegance. Very comfortable with everything you could want. Pool, patio, outdoor living area and kitchen," she replied as they paused in front of the nursery. "I'll only be a minute."

"I'll be in your room," Ashley said, walking ahead.

In the rosy glow of a small night-light Camille tiptoed across the nursery to the high-sided white crib and looked down at her sleeping son. Her heart felt squeezed, and she longed to hold Noah close. Tears stung her eyes. No matter what they did, she would lose Noah some of the time. He would have Marek's influence now. He would spend part of his life with Marek. Stephanie had been right. Momentarily, bitter regret enveloped her, and she wished she could go back and undo telling him about Noah. She reached out to touch his hand lightly, feeling the smooth, warm skin that was so soft. She had never loved anyone the way she loved Noah. Even though it would be difficult to live with, deep down she felt she had done what was right by revealing his existence to Marek.

Hopefully, Marek would be a good influence for her baby. And the Rangels deserved time with Noah just as Noah deserved a dad and his ranching heritage. She wiped her tears and took a deep breath. "I love you, sweetie," she whispered, touching a wispy lock of his hair. She wiped more tears and turned away, glancing back once at the sleeping baby.

She paused in the empty playroom, picking up a stuffed pink pig that Noah loved. Camille ran her hands over the pig while she tried to get her emotions under control. She didn't want to go to Ashley in tears. Her sisters loved Noah, too. Stephanie would be furious, but the money might calm her. Stephanie had a profound appreciation for money.

After taking a deep breath and trying to think about something else for a few minutes, she went to the master bedroom.

Ashley was curled up on the sofa, quietly waiting.

"Let me change quickly and I'll join you," Camille said. "Do you want anything to drink before we start talking? We may be here awhile."

"Now I'm getting really curious. I'll go get us both something. How about lemonade?"

"Sure. I'll be right back."

When she returned in a turquoise T-shirt and plaid pajama pants, Ashley was waiting with two tall glasses of lemonade on the table near the sofa. A plate of cookies rested between them.

"Let's hear what's up."

"Get ready for a shock. I'm talking a really big shock," she said. Ashley nodded. "He's proposed a marriage of convenience."

"No!" Ashley's brow furrowed while her eyes widened. "You turned him down, didn't you? You can't do that—"

"Ashley, listen to me. Remember, I contacted him in the first place because I wanted Noah to know his paternal family. I wanted Marek to be a father figure to Noah. I haven't given him any answer. He asked me to think it over, and I told him I would get back with him next Tuesday after talking to my family."

"You can't even give his proposal a moment's consideration. You don't have any reason to agree and you have every reason to say no."

"Do you want to hear everything or not?"

"I want to hear. Marriage is impossible. He would have far more legal claim on Noah. You'd be tied into a loveless union. Even though he is handsome, wealthy and sexy. I'll give him that much. You'd have to share Noah. Big-time. Marek wouldn't love you. He would interfere with you in every way. You can't even consider it."

"Do you want to hear his proposal or not?" Camille went through all Marek had offered. When she relayed how much money he would give them, all the color drained from Ashley's face and her mouth dropped open.

Camille grasped Ashley's hand, which was cold as ice. "Ashley. Are you all right?"

"Five million now and a million a year plus an allowance?" Ashley repeated breathlessly, sounding dazed.

"That's right. I'm trying to avoid thinking about the money, but it's impossible. With funds like that I can send you to school. I can give Mom and Dad financial help in taking care of Grandma. I can pursue my career without feeling I have to make it to be able to survive and help my family. Ashley, that money would lift a huge burden off my shoulders."

"I knew he had money, but I didn't know he had that much," she said, still sounding dazed as she stared beyond Camille.

"It will change your life and mine, for sure. It will change Noah's. He'll have a trust fund set up for him, and I'm sure it will be generous. Marek will be a father to him. We'll lose him some of the time, but definitely not all of the time. And Marek asked if you would stay as Noah's nanny. That's what he wants, and he said he would pay your salary, which, I'm certain, would be larger than what you're getting now."

"My word. I can't imagine all this, Camille. Mom will faint. She doesn't do well with surprises."

"I know. I'll break it to her slowly."

"When you started, I figured Stephanie would be furious with you for revealing Noah to Marek. Now, I don't think she will be if you tell her about the money at the same time you tell her about the proposal. You know Stephanie and money. That's the driving force in her world. How much is he going to want Noah?"

"We haven't gotten to that, but Marek keeps telling me that he wants me to be happy and doesn't want to hurt me in any way."

"You'll be a millionaire."

"Ashley, get around the money. It's a plus and you can't ignore it, but that isn't what's critical here. I think Marek should be in Noah's life. I also think a marriage of convenience might work and benefit Noah, which is the paramount criterion."

"True, but I cannot stop thinking about the possibilities the money would give us."

Camille listened to Ashley talk while part of her thoughts

were on Marek and his proposal. Was he happy with the prospects? How much of the time would he want Noah at the ranch with him? Could Ashley live in the isolation of a ranch on the Texas plains?

She didn't have answers to those questions, and she tried to focus on Ashley, who was still chattering about Marek's offer. Camille couldn't see how she could have any answer except one.

The next morning Marek sat over coffee with Jess, who had hung his hat on a hook at the door in the back entrance. Jess studied him as he sipped steaming black coffee. "What did Ginny say?"

"You can guess. She's totally opposed, thinks I'll regret getting locked into a loveless marriage. She's certain I have a lot to lose. As you can imagine, she was wild."

Jess merely nodded. When Marek's phone rang, he glanced at the number. "Here she is again. I'll have to listen to all her arguments this morning."

"Hi, Ginny," he said. He nodded. After a moment, he ended the call. "She's on the drive coming in. The whole Dalton family came with her so the girls can ride while Ginny talks to me. Frank will stay with the girls. She wants to talk to me in person. For her to drive all the way out here from Dallas is even more serious."

Jess drank the last of his coffee and stood. "That's my cue to get the horses ready. I'll see about Frank and the girls. You can deal with Ginny. She'll come around, but you'll have to listen to her vent about it. She's just looking out for you and your best interests."

"I know." Marek walked out with Jess and watched Ginny and her family spill out of their van. Jess greeted Ginny, and they talked a moment with Ginny waving her hands before she walked toward the house. Jess shook hands with Ginny's husband while the girls stood waiting for his greeting.

Frank Dalton, Ginny's husband, was a no-nonsense accountant with his own business. Marek liked him and thought he was a good match for his sister. Jess hunkered down to say hello to the little girls, and they all headed toward the barn. Ginny sailed through the back gate, her short, shaggy black hair blowing in the wind.

Marek told himself to hang on to his patience with her.

She swept into the kitchen, her face almost as red as her shirt. "Marek, have you lost your senses? You can't marry someone you don't love."

"Hi there, sis. You look a little hot and bothered. Want a cool drink?"

"No, I don't. We drove all the way out here so I can talk some sense into you. Pray she turns you down."

"Ginny, I'll have the cool drink. And I hope she accepts. I think this is the solution to the problem. I don't think it will create a bigger problem."

"And when you fall in love again?"

"There is still something called divorce if this marriage becomes a burden. But I do not expect to fall in love again. Sometimes someone falls in love for a lifetime. He loves that one person and that is the only love of his life on this earth. You don't believe that happens?"

"Maybe sometimes, but I don't think that will be the case with you. You hurt now, but you're strong and young and you'll love again."

"Is your crystal ball out in the car? You think you know me better than I know myself?"

"I don't want you locked into something where you get hurt."

He smiled at her. "Relax, Ginny. I appreciate your concern. I've thought about this and I think it's a workable solution," he said, retrieving a cold beer and opening the bottle. "Want to sit where it's comfortable?" he asked, motioning toward the living area adjoining the kitchen. "You can see the girls riding around in the corral from there."

"They brought their swimsuits because they'll be hot after they ride. They were overjoyed to get to see the horses. Marek, please do not do this. I know you will be unhappy."

"Stop worrying. I've looked at this every which way and I still think this is the best solution. I'll have some control. We'll have Noah with us far more. She'll be in Budapest this fall. If I don't do something, she'll take him to Budapest and we won't even see him all the time they're gone. I don't want to lose him. Or even be merely a tiny part of his life. He's too important to me. I think he is to you, too."

"He is, but so are you," she said, frowning. "I don't want you hurt."

"Ginny, stop worrying. I've gotten myself into this. If it doesn't work, I'll get myself out. This is an ambitious, busy woman who doesn't have time for a private life. She sings at the Metropolitan in New York next spring. Her career is rising, and she'll need help with Noah."

"She has help. Her sister is her nanny." Ginny sat staring at him, rubbing her forehead. She shook her head. "I pray you're right and you know what you're doing. She's trying to carve out a career for herself and she's been somewhat successful so far. What happens if you fall in love with her? You'll get hurt. She isn't going to settle down and give up that career."

"I would never ask her to, and I'm not going to fall in love."

"You're still suffering over your loss, but eventually you'll heal and move on. You'll hurt yourself. She will let you see Noah some without you marrying her. Please don't do this."

"I want more than brief visits with him several times a year."

"Since when did you want to become a dad?"

"You know how I love your girls."

"Yes, but you're their uncle, not their dad, which is much more demanding. It's a demanding, full-time job and you'll love that baby like you can't believe. Then, if you and Camille split, you'll really be torn. Have you thought about that?"

"Yes, but life is fraught with hazards and you just have to take some risks when you love someone whether it's a child or an adult."

She turned away to watch her girls. "You don't know what love is until a child comes into your life. Frank's life and mine revolve around the girls. You take that baby to raise part of the time and you'll love him more than you can possibly imagine. Maybe you already love him just because he's Kern's."

"Ginny, stop worrying. I want to take the chance. I want him in our lives."

Silence stretched while they studied each other. He waited patiently, certain of what he planned.

"Okay, Marek, I'll try to stop worrying and I'll stop arguing with you," she said finally. "I'm going on record though. I think you're making an enormous mistake."

"If this were turned around and Kern was in the spot I'm in and it was my baby, I think Kern would want me to do the best thing for Noah. I've mulled it over, and this seems the best solution to keep Noah in our lives."

"You might be right. When will she give you an answer?"

"Tuesday night we'll get together again. I think I'll know then, and I'll call you as soon as I do. She's talking to her sisters now."

"I can't imagine you doing this. I can't imagine her doing

it, either. Both of you have switched off your common sense. Maybe her sisters will talk her out of it."

"Stephanie will try. I'll call you Wednesday morning."

"You call me Tuesday night. I'll be a wreck. In the meantime, I'll try to think up another plan."

He smiled. "Thanks, Ginny. Tuesday night we'll know whether I'll marry Camille or not."

Tuesday night, he had butterflies in his stomach. He had made multimillion-dollar deals without a qualm, but tonight he suffered uncustomary nerves. For once in his life he didn't have a backup plan. This was it, and he could only pray she accepted. Stepping into the entrance of her condo, he experienced the same reaction as the first day he had met her, an awareness of how striking she was and the sense of energy surrounding her even as she stood still. Her hair was a midnight cascade, falling below her shoulders. Her sleeveless black dress with a scooped neckline revealed lush curves. A thin gold chain with a diamond pendant circled her throat.

"Hi," she said, smiling at him. "Come in."

"You look gorgeous," he said.

Marek could not discern any indication of her decision from her expression. He realized she was an actress as well as a singer and she hid her feelings well. She would do well in a boardroom in a high-stakes negotiation. "You asked to see Noah before we leave for the evening," she said, leading him into the living area and motioning toward the leather couch. "Have a seat, and I'll go get Noah. I won't be gone long."

"So Noah is awake and happy?" Marek suspected that with one look at her sisters he would know Camille's answer to his proposal.

"He's awake and bubbly. Stephanie has gone out for the evening, and Ashley is on the phone." She hurried out of the room to the nursery, where Ashley waited with Noah.

"Thanks, Ashley. I'll bring him back to you. Sure you don't want to come say hi?"

"No, I might start crying," she said, pushing up the sleeves to her gray sweatshirt.

"We've talked about this. The money should be some consolation."

"I worry about you. I worry about how badly you'll miss having Noah with you."

"I'll be fine. I have my career. Marek said he can change the schedule if we want to see Noah more."

"I hope he holds to that."

Camille took her son and hurried back to the front room. Marek stood by the piano, looking at sheet music. His navy suit and tie were a quiet understatement of his power and wealth. A tall, handsome and appealing man, always commanding. Was he ever at a loss or uncertain? He turned to cross the room.

"Ah, the happy baby," he said, reaching for Noah, who kicked and held out his arms.

"Do you really want to take him? Your shirt looks fresh and it's white as snow."

"I'm not fragile and my shirt washes," Marek said, taking off his coat and tossing it to the sofa. He turned to Noah.

"I think he remembers you."

"Hey, that's great. I hope so. I suspect he's happy to see everyone. So far, I haven't seen him unhappy."

"He has his moments, but most of the time, he's happy."

Marek walked away, talking to Noah, carrying him to the window to show him the outside. Then he sat on the floor with him and handed him some toys. It amazed her to watch him, the wealthy, powerful rancher dressed in his immaculate suit, tailor-made white shirt and his hand-tooled boots that could have been custom-made, while he sat on the floor playing and making goofy noises for Noah. Noah laughed, a hearty sound that made him shake all over, and she couldn't keep from laughing with him.

"Why will grown people do anything to get a baby to laugh?"

"Got me, but it's fun. You can't keep from laughing in return," Marek said, making another silly sound and laughing with Noah. Her heart squeezed while her pulse jumped. Marek's appeal soared when he laughed. Creases bracketed his mouth and his even white teeth flashed. Her heart was definitely in for a bumpy ride.

Finally, he stood. "I'll give him to you. Another night we'll play longer."

"I'll take him back to Ashley. Just a minute and we can go."

She hurried out of the room, holding Noah tightly in her arms, wondering whether she was making the right decision or not. After tonight, there wouldn't be any turning back.

Just as before, they went in a limo to his Dallas home, where they sat outside with drinks. He removed his navy suit jacket and tie as he had the last time. While she watched him, it occurred to her to wonder about his handsome appeal. Was she in any danger of falling in love? He sat close, facing her. He set both drinks on a glass table.

"I've waited long enough, and we're alone now," Marek said. "What's your answer? Will you marry me?"

Four

Her insides roiled and her palms became damp even though her hands felt icy as she gazed into his brown eyes.

Taking a deep breath, she nodded. "Yes, I will."

He closed his eyes briefly, then opened them. He pulled her up and gave her a light hug. "Thank you," he said in a voice that sounded choked with emotion.

He smelled of citrus and sandalwood and the fresh cottony scent of his immaculate dress shirt. He was warm and tall, and his arms around her felt reassuring. He leaned away a fraction to look down at her and her only thought at that moment was how handsome he was. "We'll make this work, Camille," he said in a husky voice. A pang racked her because his emotional reaction was not due to her, but to her baby.

"I don't want to fall in love," she whispered, biting back the words that if she did, he would break her heart.

His dark eyes widened and then narrowed as he gazed at her, a look that became more intense. She felt as if he was seeing her as a woman for the first time. He inhaled deeply, and a hard look came to his features while a muscle worked in his jaw.

"Forget what I said," she said, stepping out of his embrace, walking away from him to put distance between them and to keep him from seeing the flush of embarrassment in her cheeks. "My heart is in my career and Noah, and, right now, I can't imagine us being together a lot of the time." Her words spilled out, sounding rushed to her, and she felt foolish. Trying to get a grip and be less emotional, she finally faced him.

"Thank you, Camille," he said, looking composed again. "We can start working out details, put down what we want in a prenuptial agreement that we can turn over to our lawyers to finalize. How's that?"

"Sounds fine." She returned to get her glass of wine and sit in a green-cushioned teak lawn chair. He sat facing her and sipped his drink. "I'll get a tablet to make notes as we talk about what we want." He left to get papers from a cabinet and returned to hand a tablet to her. She looked down at proposed schedules.

"I have schedules worked out, but you know your bookings and shows. This is just something to start from. Also, as soon as we sign the papers, I'll have money transferred to you."

"That's sort of staggering," she said, unable to imagine that she would soon become a millionaire. Her gaze ran over him, his broad shoulders, his capable, well-shaped hands.

"We'll be married, Camille. As far as I'm concerned, your money is yours to do with as you please. I'll pay your expenses and your housing, all that sort of thing. Just get Stephanie to keep accurate records."

"That's very generous considering how much money you're giving me. I earn a good living so far."

"I'll treat you the same as I would a wife in the fullest

sense of the word as far as finances and that sort of thing are concerned. How are your sisters and your parents with this arrangement?"

"Ashley is worried about Noah. The money means a lot because she's saved and scraped together for her education. Stephanie is practical enough to accept this. She does not like sharing Noah, but she is going to like the money immensely. She sees the possibility of having her own business, perhaps picking up more clients than she has now."

"Good. What about Ashley staying on as nanny?"

"Ashley will be nanny at first. Later, if you can find a good nanny, she would like to go to college full-time and finish her education."

"Sure. Tell her to let me know when to start looking for a new nanny."

"I haven't told my parents yet about the money. I'd rather they meet you first and feel this is a marriage of two people in love. Otherwise, they may not get past the money and may never be able to see the reasons I want this for Noah as a tie to his father."

Stretching out his legs, he looked relaxed, as if they were discussing the latest movie or electronic breakthrough. Watching him, no one would guess he was making life-changing decisions. The evening had become surreal. She couldn't imagine the changes, yet they were happening. Even more impossible to imagine—she would soon marry a man she didn't love and barely knew. She let her gaze roam down the length of him, and her pulse raced. He appealed to her, and she hadn't really had a man in her life in a long time. To her regret, she had a strong physical response to him. Already, if he came close or if there was physical contact with him, her pulse jumped. With her life focused on her career, she didn't want complications by becoming emotionally entangled with Marek.

"Well, what we've both avoided and what we have to work out is how will we share Noah? I've thought about all sorts of ways to divide the time. I've come up with something that's a start. We can change it completely so that each of us finds it workable."

"Right now, this part is difficult to imagine," she admitted, fighting back tears because she felt as if she stood on the verge of losing Noah. For a panicky moment, she wanted to change her mind, but there was no turning back time and events. "The first thing I'll do when I get home tonight is go see him. I miss him when I'm away from him for just hours," she said, struggling to hang on to her emotions. "Days are impossible to think about."

"The first little bit will be the hardest, and we won't jump into a schedule the minute we marry," he promised, taking her hand. "Stop worrying so much, Camille. I'll work with you on this and maybe we can't do a lot at first while he's tiny. Besides, some of the time, you and I will be under the same roof and you'll have him as much as ever. The difference will be I'll be living with you, too."

A shiver spiraled through her as his words echoed in her thoughts. How vastly her life would change. Locked into a loveless union, she would spend part of her time on his ranch. She couldn't imagine that. His thumb lightly rubbed the back of her hand while his brown eyes hid his feelings. Yet why should he be emotional over this proposition—it was his idea and what he wanted desperately. Her acceptance of his proposal was worth millions to him, so all he hid was his desire to convince her to cooperate.

"Let's face it, Camille," he said in a softer tone. "We have a positive physical response to each other now. That's a plus any way you look at it."

Her heartbeat increased a notch. "I didn't know you noticed."

"I've more than noticed since the first day I met you," he said. "We'll get along," he added in a huskier tone that surprised her, a tone that made his words sound as if he referred to a physical relationship. "We'll just do a day here and a day there so you get more accustomed to this and see if it's workable," he said, getting back to the matter at hand. "When we're in the same town, we'll be in the same living quarters so there will be no problem. At some point, I'd like him a week out of each month. You will get him the other three weeks. That's not even half the time. How does that sound to you?" he asked. He leaned forward, his elbows on his knees. Marek once again sounded businesslike, in control of the situation.

Trying to avoid thinking about Noah, she picked up the calendar. "I'll be in Budapest in the fall, so you will have him two weeks out of those months."

"I said at some point. For now, he should stay with you while he's under a year old."

She stared at him, feeling as if a huge weight had lifted. Her pulse began to race with rising joy. "Do you really mean that?"

"Of course. When you're in New Mexico, you'll have him all of the time because we're just starting and he's too little to be away from you. We'll ease into this. As he grows, the schedule will change anyway."

She felt as if sunshine had just spilled over her. "You didn't say that before. I'm so relieved. I've been trying to imagine him in Texas when I'm in Santa Fe and I can't even bear to think about it. That is a wonderful wedding gift. Marek, I'm overjoyed," she said, giving him a squeeze.

He laughed in one of his rare moments with a flash of white teeth. "I think you are far happier over this news about Noah than over your ring or the money or any material gain."

"Of course, I am. You should understand why."

"I should have come to this conclusion from the start," he said, still smiling, and her happiness rose. "I want Noah to be a Rangel, and I hope he loves the ranch. Kern loved ranching."

"In our weekend together, I got that much from him, so I feel I'm giving Noah part of his dad by our marriage and seeing that he grows up knowing the ranch life. It's a relief to know he won't start living there without me when he's so tiny. If I find any of what we do difficult to live with, you'll hear from me about it."

"I'd want to. I want something we can both live with."

"Right now, even when he's older, I can't imagine him gone for almost a month."

"We'll work into long stays gradually. You can come visit anytime you want, and if that's bad, I can bring him to see you or we can try to work something else out."

He loosened his tie and pulled it off, unbuttoning the top button of his shirt. Her mouth went dry watching him. He was way too appealing. She looked away, reminding herself to guard her heart carefully. There was no room in her life for love right now, and Marek was definitely not the man to be the object of her affections. Not until he could love again—if that time ever came.

"We need to pay off your lease and move you to my Dallas home before the wedding. You, Noah, your sisters, everything. I want you to look tomorrow at my house and begin to decide which rooms to make over for you and your family, a nursery, a music room—the whole thing."

"That's monumental."

"Not at all. We'll get it done," he said with supreme confidence. "If the redecorating isn't finished when you move in, it won't matter."

"I feel as if I'm caught in a whirlwind."

He smiled. "You're caught in a marriage of convenience

that I think will make us both happy. I've been sort of caught in a whirlwind since you entered my life," he said, and she laughed.

"No way. You're insulated."

"You're beginning to bring me back to life, whether I want it or not." He picked up the calendar to hand it to her. "I'd like to marry as soon as you feel you can. We can have a big church wedding or something small or something somewhere in between. I want the wedding to be whatever you would like and make it as much a real wedding as possible because we might stay together."

"We might stay together," she repeated, shaking her head. "This is a dream and I think I'll wake up from it. I can't imagine so much of this. Staying together? That seems totally impossible. I think one of us will fall in love with someone else and that will be that."

"No matter what we plan, you can't foresee the future. You never expected this to happen, and neither did I. That first day I was in total shock. That morning I had a list of other things I had planned for my day, my week and my month. When you left my office, my life had changed forever."

"Actually, there we had the same experience. My life changed just as drastically. For me, though, it was for the second time. The first big change was when I met your brother."

"Kern and I were so damn close. I still miss him every day," Marek said, looking away, his voice changing, becoming harsh and cold. He spoke as if talking to himself, and she wondered if he had forgotten her presence and withdrawn into his shell again.

He turned to her. "Let's get back to thinking about a wedding."

"I haven't given any thought to a wedding. I've been so busy thinking about Noah." She studied the calendar. "Under the circumstances, I prefer a small wedding with our families and very closest friends."

"Whatever you want," he replied. "Big or small, I'll pay all the expenses and we can pull the event together quickly. I'd like it as soon as possible because it would be better if we can get settled somewhat before you take off for New Mexico. I'll lease or buy a place in Santa Fe this summer. You can select it and then I can come when I want to."

For the first time, she realized he might be in her life far more than she had expected. "You don't mind leaving your ranch?"

"I'd rather be on the ranch, but I do have others who'll keep it running smoothly. I can rely on Jess as much as I can on myself." Marek sipped his drink and set down his glass.

"Do you care for more wine?"

"No, thank you. My head is spinning enough over all the changes from your proposal."

He sat back and studied her. "We're going too fast for you. Want to stop and think about what we've said for a couple of days and then go back to planning?"

"I'm tempted," she said, relieved he wasn't pushing this on her too much. "We might as well go ahead. If the plans get to be too much for me, I'll tell you. These are monumental changes coming one right after another, like a series of wrecks all in one day."

His eyes narrowed. "I hope it isn't as harsh as a series of wrecks. I hope you can gain more than just money out of this."

"Noah will gain more—he'll get a dad who, hopefully, will love him."

"I already love him. All I have to do is look at him and think about his dad. He's a happy baby, so that makes him doubly lovable."

She looked away, having another moment when her emotions threatened to overwhelm her. "I can maintain better control on a stage than I can here."

"That's different. You can walk away from that without it tearing up your life."

Startled that he understood, she turned back to look at him. "You're perceptive, thank heavens," she admitted. "That makes me feel a tiny bit better."

"Good," he said gently. He placed his hand on her cheek lightly. "Camille, we'll get through this. Just always tell me and I'll tell you if something isn't working."

Again he surprised her and also made her feel better. "Thank you," she whispered, looking into his dark eyes and wondering about the future.

Picking up the calendar, he studied it. "A small wedding should be easy. How about the last Saturday in April?"

"Two weeks and a few days?" She laughed, her worry transformed to amusement over his ridiculous expectations. She shook her head. "That seems impossible, even for a small wedding. I'm free right now from any performances, so I agree it should be before I perform in Dallas and definitely before I go to New Mexico, but two weeks? It can't be done. I'm sure I can't even book the church with that short of notice."

"If necessary, we can marry at my ranch. There are plenty of places. Remember, don't worry about expenses. I'm paying and I can get people moving," he said in a determined tone.

"I'm sure you can," she replied, looking at the calendar he was holding. He had well-shaped hands, strong wrists. His French cuffs had gold links that flashed when he moved. Returning her attention to the calendar, she studied it. "It's April. How about the second Saturday in May? That is really fast for a wedding."

"How about the first Saturday in May?" he asked. "I

promise, we can pull this together. I'll give you all the help you want."

She stared at the date and finally nodded. "If you think that's possible, I guess that will be all right."

"I know it's possible."

She glanced up at him. "You're supremely confident, but I imagine you get what you want the majority of the time."

"No. I didn't with Jillian and Kern. But some things are doable if you have the resources."

"Or the determination," she added quietly.

"We're doing well together, Camille. This is a good sign," he said. He patted her hand. "See, it's working."

Again, his slightest, casual touch, a touch that was meaningless to him, stirred unwanted responses in her. Was she getting herself into a situation that would hurt deeply later? This change with Noah was unwanted, foisted on her. Falling in love would be equally as unwanted and complicated. Realizing that he was saying something to her, she tried to get her mind back on their discussion.

"I'll need to get the church, let my sisters be bridesmaids, even though I want to keep this small. I need to take you home to meet my family."

"It's fine with me however you want to handle it. They're your family. Except you didn't tell them everything, so they had no part in the decision you made."

"Correct. I think they would see all this differently. And they don't fully understand the job or career that I have, either. They like my singing and are proud of me, but I know they wish I had a regular job where I lived in Saint Louis or one particular place and went to an office each day."

"They'll get used to your career as it grows. So we go meet Mom and Dad."

"And brother and grandmother. What about your parents? You said they're not very involved now with you and your sister."

"They've said they will be here as soon as they can. Mom hates flying, but she'll do so. They'll be here for the wedding, I'm sure."

"You're still hurting over your loss. We barely know each other. Frankly, I prefer to put a physical relationship on hold. If we stay together the time will come when we might want to have one, but at this point, there are a lot of uncertainties and we're not in love."

"Whatever you want. We should make decisions about a honeymoon."

"A honeymoon seems foolish under the circumstances. We have a business arrangement."

"One, for distant relatives and friends, it will be simpler because everything will appear normal. Also, we can take three or four days off and get to know each other. We can take Noah if you want. As far as I'm concerned, that would be fun. Or if you'd like just a few days away from the baby, your lessons and your practice, we can be the only ones. Actually, it might be wise for us to get to know each other a little better. We won't be able to as much if we have Noah."

"I'll think about being away from him. Three days is definitely the longest I want to be gone."

"That's fine. What would you enjoy doing for a few days together?" he asked.

"If we're going to do what I want, it would be magical to take just a couple of days, just a weekend, and go to some tropical place, perhaps the Caribbean. Somewhere that has palm trees and an ocean. If we go with Noah along, I'll be willing to stay longer. Without Noah, I don't want to be gone more than a day or two there plus a day going and a day to return."

"That's easy enough."

"Frankly, I've been to Europe and will be going again. I've been to Russia and various cities in the U.S. I've never been to the tropics."

"The lady is not only beautiful, but easy to please. The tropics it is. If the weather is good, and it should be, a villa on Grand Cayman in the Caribbean might be the perfect place. Do you want just us or everyone?"

She laughed. "Since we're not telling the world that this will be a marriage of convenience, I suggest we go alone," she replied. "Just two days in the tropics with a beach and I'll be happy and store it in my memories forever."

"We'll take four days. Get married on Saturday, head for the tropics, stay two days, fly back to Texas." He sat forward. "We'll be going to an island where we can choose from several things to do the night we get there. We can go dancing, attend a show."

"You just mentioned a villa. Let's just stay there. It's all new to me, and I'll be happy just to sit and relax."

"You're easy to please, Camille," he said again. She was a beautiful woman and she did turn heads anytime they were in public. He thought of Noah and, as always, his nerves calmed. This was the right thing to do and the only thing to get Noah really into the lives of the Rangels. "Let's go to dinner now some place where we can dance. We'll let off steam and celebrate working this out." Without waiting for an answer, he stood and pulled a cell phone out of his pocket to make a call and get reservations for two.

Dynamic was another trait she could add to his description. He had taken charge and barreled through everything quickly, efficiently in a lot of ways. Would she have charge of her life from now on, or would Marek Rangel constantly influence it?

Within the hour they were seated in a private club overlooking the city with glass windows giving a floor-to-ceiling view. Steaks had been ordered, and Marek stood. "Let's dance," he said. On the dance floor he took her into his arms, holding her lightly. She was more aware of each contact with him, of her hand in his. The fact that she would soon be his wife was as impossible a prospect as the realization she would soon be a millionaire.

"I'm pleased by the prospects of marrying, seeing Noah grow up and being part of his life. I hope you are."

"I have mixed feelings, and my sisters do, too. We're all scared how we'll feel the first time we're away from Noah."

"That's natural. When we start, we'll keep those times very brief."

"Thank you. I feel much better knowing separation won't be so long. So, Jess and your sister think this is a good plan?"

"Jess does. I told you that. Ginny is not so enthusiastic. Actually, Ginny is worried about me, which is ridiculous, but she's my big sister and sometimes that pops out. She calmed down some after we talked and is a little better about accepting our marriage."

"Our marriage. I won't believe it's happening even after we've walked down the aisle."

"Camille, if you ever do fall in love with someone, come tell me."

As they danced to an old ballad, she gazed into his eyes, seeing the earnest look, realizing he didn't have any expectations that they would fall in love. "I will tell you if I think you need to know," she answered.

He shook his head. "Tell me whether you think I need to know or not. I don't want to hold you to something if you're unhappy. Promise me you'll tell me."

"No. You won't win this one. If I think you need to know, I'll tell you."

He frowned slightly, looking over her head in the distance as if watching something far away. "I'm not happy with that answer."

"Put it out of your mind. Tonight there's no need in worrying about something that might happen."

Her gaze was held by his as he gave her a searching look. "Just remember, I tried to get you to promise to tell me."

"I will remember," she said, knowing she always would. How much time would they spend together? Questions constantly ran through her thoughts about her future. Could she avoid falling in love? Would he ever really notice her or get over his grief and come back into the world?

The next number was fast and it felt good to dance with him, a silly tune that made everyone on the dance floor smile, let go and enjoy themselves. Her gaze was locked with Marek's, and he looked happy, but why wouldn't he, when he had her promise to give him everything he wanted? He had let go, dancing with zest, making sexy moves.

She danced around him. At the end, he caught her hand, spun her around and dipped her low, holding her. She clung to him because she was off balance as he leaned down so her hair touched the floor. Both of them laughed when he swung her up.

"You're beautiful, Camille," he said lightly, smiling at her with his even white teeth showing. His rare smiles always heightened his appeal.

"Thank you. I didn't know you've ever really noticed me," she replied.

"I've noticed you," he answered. "Ready to go back to the table?"

As they were seated the waiter appeared to open a bottle of champagne, an expensive brand she had only had once before in her life.

"We're celebrating your acceptance of my proposal."

"Congratulations," the waiter said to Marek, then turned to smile at her. "Best wishes, miss."

"Thank you," she replied, laughing as he walked away and Marek raised his glass.

"Here's to a successful union for both of us. May it fulfill needs and bless everyone involved."

They touched glasses with a faint ringing sound of crystal.

"Marek, there are only two people involved in a marriage," she pointed out drily.

He shook his head. "There are a lot of people involved. It will change other lives. Noah's, Ashley's, Stephanie's, your family, my family. This wedding definitely will touch more lives. And this is a celebration because I hope, for one and all, the effects will be great."

"I agree to that one."

"May your joy be full, Camille, and your career soar."

They touched glasses again, and she took another tiny sip of bubbly champagne.

She held up her glass. "May your joy be full, too, Marek, and may joy replace grief and give you peace," she said, touching his glass lightly, watching him over the rim of her glass as she sipped. Her heart drummed. She couldn't keep from glancing at his mouth, wondering about his kisses, wondering whether he would ever really kiss her. She looked up to find him watching her, but he still had that faint crooked smile and she suspected he had not noticed her studying his mouth, much less seen anything in her expression when she had looked up.

He leaned across the linen-covered table, moving a vase of roses out of his way. "I'm beginning to look forward to our tropical getaway, to being alone with you and getting to know you," he said softly, stirring more tingles.

"You're almost flirting, Marek," she said lightly.

"We might as well have a little fun," he answered. "And you'll be my bride soon."

"Sounds impossible. I hope your plans work as you expect. Such upheaval and monumental changes are scary," she replied, thinking about having to part with Noah sometimes, as well as about Marek's promise to keep her happy. He would try in every way except one. His heart was deeply guarded, locked away. Would he ever let go and love again?

He pulled a card out of his shirt pocket and held it out to her. "I'll go with you tomorrow to this jeweler. I can put a limo at your disposal, so after the jewelry store you can shop for a wedding dress. If you prefer, I can fly you to New York to select your dress."

"I'll find a dress in Dallas," she said, thinking this would never be as important as it would have been had she been in love.

"This jeweler is good. You can work with him on the engagement and wedding ring you'd like to have. Do not worry about the price. That's why I'm going. I want to make sure you spend at least a certain amount, but you might as well select your ring."

"I don't need some fabulous ring."

"I want you to have a 'fabulous' ring for marrying me and bringing Noah into my life. Kern would definitely want you to have a spectacular ring. We might as well discuss this now instead of in the jewelry store. Don't hold back. I want you to get what you want. I mean that. I want you to have at least an eight-carat diamond. You can go from there."

"Marek, that is an enormous diamond that isn't necessary or logical. It doesn't represent our love."

"It represents my gratitude," he said. Continuing to hold her hand, he sat close and she looked at the slight curl of his thick, dark lashes that framed his eyes and added to his handsome looks. "If we were deeply in love, I would select your ring and surprise you with it. Under the circumstances, I thought you might as well get what you want. I want it to be nice. I want it extravagant, a constant reminder of my gratitude to you. You can select a design working with this jeweler. He's excellent."

"Thank you," she replied, feeling touched that he had made such a huge effort to convey how grateful he was. A tiny twinge of guilt fluttered because she knew if she could go back and undo telling him about Noah, she might do so.

The day would have come when Noah would ask about his father, and she would have to tell him, but not while he was a baby. She might have waited the first formative years until he was in school and she was separated from him anyway. At the same time, her guilt would have been greater because this way, she felt she was doing the right thing for Noah. He should benefit all his life from this union.

They sat back down when their steaks had been served, but Camille had no appetite. The monumental changes she faced were all she could think about. To her relief, they both lapsed into silence and Marek didn't seem compelled to talk or try to entertain her.

"You're worried, aren't you?" he said finally.

"I can't keep from thinking about all of the plans we've made. I've been accustomed to goals and schedules. Suddenly I'm facing a whole new way of living."

"You're not eating. I didn't want all this to upset you."

"It's just different. You're not exactly wolfing down your dinner, either," she said and received a faint smile.

"Want to dance again? Would you rather go home?"

Relieved, she nodded. "I would rather go home. This has been quite a night."

In a short time they were in the limo headed to her condo. "Can you go at ten in the morning to look at rings?"

"Yes," she said.

He half turned toward her and folded her hand in his. "If you want to call me during the night, I don't care what hour, go ahead. If you have questions, worries, let me know."

"Thanks. I have a million questions. Will this work out? How will I get through giving up Noah? Will he be happy?"

"Ashley will still be with him."

"Right now, I'd rather be his nanny and have her be the singer."

"Do either of your sisters sing?"

"No. Stephanie, absolutely not. Ashley has a nice voice but not a strong one, and she doesn't have the drive to want this. She loves children, wants to be a teacher. We're all rather different."

"As different, I guess, as Kern, Ginny and I are. I wish I could take away your worry, but I can't. The money was supposed to help. This goes way beyond money, which becomes insignificant."

She had to smile. "Millions do not become insignificant," she said. "Well, maybe the thrill of the money does diminish next to the rest," she admitted.

"I know it does. It shows in every way. If I told you I'd changed my mind and didn't care and was going to stay out of your life and take my money, your only feeling would be relief. I don't have to ask if I'm right."

She looked outside at the busy thoroughfare and again had to fight tears. He was right. The millions meant nothing next to letting him have so much of Noah.

They rode the rest of the way to her condo in silence. On her porch, he placed his hands on her shoulders. "Camille, I'll repeat—I'm thrilled beyond measure over your acceptance of my proposal. I promise to try to keep you and your sisters happy. I'm thrilled and excited over the prospects and we'll get along in this quasi marriage."

"I hope so," she said. "I pray this is good for Noah. That's the one thing I really cling to. The money will benefit me and my family in several ways, but it's the thought that you'll be good for Noah that really makes this acceptable. It's what I wanted in the first place."

"I'll do everything in my power to make it good for him." Marek's brown eyes were unfathomable as he studied her. "When we wed, we'll kiss in church. I don't want that to be our first kiss," he said, his dark gaze focusing on her mouth. Her heart drummed so violently she hoped he couldn't hear it. His announcement that he intended to kiss her caused every nerve to come alive. Why was it so enormously un-settling? His kiss should be meaningless.

As his arm circled her waist, she could barely get her breath. He drew her closer, and she rested her hands lightly against his upper arms.

When he leaned down, she closed her eyes, tilting her face up to his. His mouth covered hers lightly, then pressing more firmly, warm, sexy, tempting. Her lips parted and then his did while his tongue slipped into her mouth. The first stroke changed their relationship for her forever. No more was he a new acquaintance becoming closely involved with her. He was an appealing, sexy man she would be entering into an intimate relationship with. Slowly, with deliberation, he kissed her while he drew her up against him. Feeling the bulge of hard biceps beneath her hands, she stood quietly. Leaning over her, he tightened his arm around her.

She kissed him in return, tumbling into an abyss that made her stomach flip and her heart pound faster. With-out thinking about what she was doing, she slipped her arm around his neck, and then she realized how she had re-sponded. She leaned away and gasped for breath.

"Now we've kissed," she whispered, feeling stunned be-cause his kiss had been sexy, possessive—a hot kiss that conveyed he cared while that wasn't actually the situation.

He gave her another inscrutable look and said nothing.

"Good night, Marek."

"I'll see you for dinner tomorrow night and we can firm up plans, call parents and whoever we need to tell while we're together. I'm happy, Camille," he said, smiling at her.

He turned away to get into the waiting limo while she went inside, her heart pounding. His kiss had melted her, shaken her and set her on fire. Could she live with this? How long would it be a marriage of convenience only?

She would lose Noah part of the time. Now another threat loomed that she might fall in love with Marek and complicate her life in every way possible. She had known that was a risk, but it had seemed slight. His kiss had smashed that opinion to bits. Her lips tingled, and she shook her head.

"I can't fall in love with him," she whispered. Yet her heartbeat still raced from his kiss and she would remember forever the look in his eyes afterward, a heated, possessive look, a look that clearly expressed that he saw her as a desirable woman.

"I thought I heard you," Ashley said, coming into the hall from the family room. She was in turquoise pajamas and a matching robe.

"I'm going to marry him," Camille announced as if trying to convince herself. "I accepted. You know that's what we decided."

Ashley shook her head. "I hope you know what you're doing. I'll be with Noah, but you won't be."

"I'm going to be with him more than I thought at first."

"All that money, Camille. I can't even imagine our lives."

"I think you'll want to go to school before long. Maybe by next fall. We'll find a nanny. There's bound to be another good one in the world."

"Let's just take this a little bit at a time. This will change the lives of everyone in the family."

"Where's Stephanie?"

"I'm here," she said from the shadows, coming into the hallway. "I heard you accepted."

"I'll go out with him tomorrow night and we'll call our parents to make the official announcement."

Ashley walked to Camille to hug her lightly. "I'll pray this works out."

"It has to be good for everyone. We're not losing Noah and he's gaining a dad and we're all improving financially."

"That's an understatement," Stephanie said. "I think sleep has gone for tonight for all three of us. While you go change, Ashley and I will get some hot chocolate. We can hear your plans and maybe help you with some."

"Thanks, Steph," Camille said, smiling at her sister and thankful that Stephanie was beginning to accept Marek and the situation. "I'll need help with plans. We're aiming for a wedding in about three weeks. He'll pay for everything, he said. I think our whole family will be all for this. If they aren't, Marek will win them over."

"I think you're right. That first night I didn't think I ever wanted to see him again. Now I can't help but feel like this may benefit Noah and everyone else. Hurry and change so we can talk," Stephanie said.

"Sure," Camille replied and left the room. As she changed, all she could think about was his kiss that had set her heart pounding. It had been sexy, hot and had made her want more. Had Marek felt anything?

At home Marek shed his coat and tie and unbuttoned his shirt as he went to the desk in his bedroom. He thought about Noah, remembering holding him and looking into his lively eyes. He already loved the baby, and he could imagine how Camille must feel.

He remembered holding her in his arms tonight when they

kissed. He dropped his pen and leaned back to think about her. Her kiss had shaken him because it had stirred him. For the first time since his loss, he had stopped feeling numb. Numbness had been replaced by desire, lust really. That had given him a shock. Because of her kiss, he had no doubt that they could have a successful physical relationship. Would this marriage work? He had been so positive with her, but deep down he now had as many unanswered questions as she did.

The question startled him because up until tonight he had thought about going into this marriage only as something that would revolve around Noah. After their kiss tonight, that expectation had flown away. There would be a physical relationship between them. He was sure of it, and he already wanted it.

Would he fall in love with her? He shook his head even though he wasn't talking to anyone. He wouldn't love again. He was as certain of that as ever. But lust was another thing. Could she handle that? As swiftly as the question rose in his mind, the knowledge that she could reassured him. She was tied to only two things: Noah and her career. Since she didn't want to fall in love, she would be guarding against it as much as he.

He had thought he was in no hurry to rush into an intimate relationship, but her kiss had changed that. Desire was palpable, strong, a torment. With a deep breath, he picked up his pen and began to list what he needed to do in the next few days.

In minutes he again was thinking back to kissing her tonight. For a few moments he was lost in a fantasy about making love to her, holding her close. With an effort he tried to get back to things he needed to do.

He would be with her tomorrow night to make plans together and to tell their families. They could get on Skype and it would be almost like being together. His gaze fell on his brother's picture, and he picked up the snapshot. Kern had his cocky grin and stood beside his favorite horse.

"Brother, I wish you could see your son. He's a great little kid. He's happy all the time and a good baby, but he has a little look in his eyes like you had plenty of times. He's going to be like you," Marek said quietly, getting a knot in his throat and wishing Kern had lived to see Noah. "At least you knew about him. I imagine you were planning to marry Camille and you probably had absolutely no doubt whatsoever that you could talk her into it. Kern, I'm sorry for the way things turned out, but I'll do my best with Noah."

Marek wiped his eyes. He missed his brother so often. Such a waste! He pulled off his shirt, feeling restless, wishing he had someone to talk to for a while. He wondered what time Camille went to bed. The thought of her stretched out in bed set his pulse racing. She wanted to wait on a physical relationship, but he suspected neither of them would wait long. If he had his preference, they would not wait at all. Just the thought set his pulse racing faster. He knew nothing about her except the facts of her background that he had gleaned from what she'd told him and the little on the web about her. She wasn't heavily into social media and neither was he, so he hadn't learned much there.

In slightly over three weeks he would be a married man—married to a woman he barely knew. The idea astounded him.

Two weeks later Marek's cell phone jingled and he answered to listen to his sister.

"Mom and Dad are so worried about you and what you're doing."

"Don't let them get to you. The paternity test indicated Noah is Kern's baby. I'm doing what I want. I think it will work out."

They were both tense about the upcoming evening. "I'll

see you at the party tonight," he said, thinking about the engagement party that was being held by his parents' dinner club and oldest friends.

"Okay, little brother. I just want you happy. Noah is a cute little fellow and he does look like Kern."

"Whether he looks like Kern or not, Noah is Kern's, Ginny. Could you let him go now?"

"No. You win. See you tonight."

"Ahh, that's my sis." He ended the call and left for the corral, thinking about the wedding. He still did not expect to love again. To love was to risk your heart, and he would never go through the kind of hurt he had experienced after losing Jillian. That was vastly different from lusting after someone. Camille knew this, and she knew what to expect from him. She was completely aware that love would never be part of the equation. Still, he wanted to make love to her. He wanted her in his arms, in his bed. He wanted her as his wife in the fullest sense. Thinking about her aroused him, and he glanced at his watch, counting the hours until he would see her.

Walking into the barn, he found Jess with his head under the hood of a truck.

"What's wrong with the pickup?"

"Nothing I can't fix," Jess said. He straightened. "They giving you a hard time?"

"Yes. Mom and Dad are worried about me rushing into a marriage. They're interested in Noah, but feel I can work out a better arrangement. I've had a call from Ginny about their opinion."

"Do *you* think you are making a mistake?"

"No. No matter how I look at it, I don't. You've seen Noah, and we all know he's Kern's baby. I can't just see him a few times a year."

"Kern's little boy, growing up here—I don't see how you can go wrong with him growing up as part of the family."

"Both Camille and I want him to have this ranching legacy."

"Amen to that. 'Course, you're tying your life to hers and hers to you, but that should work out."

"I think it will. Can I help with this?" Marek asked, leaning over the truck.

"It's a dirty job," Jess said.

"I take that as a yes. Give me the wrench, and you take a break."

"Won't argue with that one," Jess said, handing Marek his wrench and stepping away to sit on bales of hay.

Marek was soon absorbed in the truck, glad to find something that occupied his thoughts, thinking it would be a long day until he could pick up Camille for the party.

"Wedding will be here before you know it, so you better be sure," Jess said.

"The sooner the better," Marek replied. "I want to get this over with and put an end to the arguments. As soon as my tux is done, I'm ready for a wedding. I hope Camille is, too."

Five

Dressed in a tailored white silk dress with a skirt that ended below her knees, Camille stood poised to walk up the aisle in a small chapel in the Saint Louis church she had attended all her life. Her arm was looped through her father's, and he smiled at her. "You look beautiful. I hope you're happy."

"I will be, Dad," she said, watching Ashley walk up the aisle.

"This isn't what we'd hoped for you when Mom and I talked about all of you growing up and marrying, but if you're all right with it, we will be, too. As long as you're sure you're not doing it for the money."

"Absolutely not. The money is a plus, but I've tried to keep that from influencing my decision. This is about Noah."

"I hope you mean that. Camille, if this marriage doesn't work, then get out of it," Anthony Avanole said solemnly. "You'll have enough money to invest it and never touch it.

Use the interest from it and what you have if the amount grows. It'll be there to give back to Marek if you need to."

"I know, Dad," she said, looking at the tall, handsome man who stood waiting at the altar and within moments would be her husband. "Marek and I think this marriage will work. Time and again, I've been over all the reasons."

"The money is a blessing for you and for all of us. It will change our lives, but I don't want it at the cost of your happiness."

She shook her head. "It won't be. I won't stay in the relationship if it's unhappy or not the best for Noah, for all of us." The marriage still dazed her as much as the ring on her finger. She glanced down at her hand as she held the large bouquet of white orchids, lilies and white roses. Her eight-carat diamond with sapphires and diamonds along the gold band sparkled on her finger. The contradictions in her wedding were as numerous as in Marek's personality. A small wedding, an enormous bouquet and a huge, dazzling diamond. A honeymoon for two people who were almost strangers. She looked again at Marek, feeling her pulse racing. Jess was best man because Pete Rangel, Marek's father, had asked Marek to let someone stand in for him because of his crutches. His dad had been happy that Marek had asked him, even when he could not accept.

When Camille had asked Marek about it earlier, he had made it clear to her that he was happy to have Jess as his best man.

"It's time," the wedding planner said, and Camille and her dad started the walk up the aisle. As she neared Marek, she saw the somber look on his face, a look she recognized. He was fighting his emotions, and she could imagine he was thinking about his fiancée and the wedding he had expected to have.

She hurt for him, wishing she could erase his ache, knowing no one could. He stepped to her side to take her hand, his dark eyes unreadable. He smiled, but it was perfunctory.

She went through the ceremony, repeating her vows, too aware she was taking an enormous risk as well as aware of Marek's pain.

The moment the minister said, "You may kiss the bride," warmth returned to Marek's eyes as he focused on her. His kiss was light, but the look he gave her was reassuring.

When they turned to face the guests and their minister introduced them as Mr. and Mrs. Marek Rangel, her parents smiled at her and her mother dabbed her eyes. Marek's parents smiled, even though Marek's mother also had tears.

Marek took her arm to walk up the aisle, and she smiled with relief that the ceremony had ended.

They had pictures with both of their families. Even though it was a small wedding, there were more guests than she had originally thought they would have. They constantly talked to guests, and it wasn't until Marek began the first dance with her that she was alone with him. He held her lightly, smiling at her, but it was a strained smile. A muscle worked in his jaw and she hurt for him, certain he was thinking of his fiancée.

"You look beautiful today," he said. His voice sounded labored, and she would be thankful when the reception was over and they could get away.

"Thank you. You look handsome, and your pain doesn't show very much," she said, wishing she could do something to help him.

"I'm all right." He glanced beyond her, looking around the large ballroom. "Our security is tight and I don't think there are any unwanted people looking for pictures or a story."

"The security is the best ever."

"You're as calm as a summer morning. But then you're accustomed to going on stage and hiding what you feel."

"I've made my decision, and I'm hoping for the best. Noah

has been on his best behavior all day as if he senses something special is happening." Marek's slight smile looked real this time, and she relaxed a little. "Perhaps someday we'll dance and you'll be delighted that I'm the person in your arms."

"I am happy over this, Camille. In more ways than you can guess. You've brought me out of the grief I had sunk into. I think this union is going to be great for all of us."

"That's what I'm counting on, too."

"We'll do all right together, because we each have our own lives and we're really not going to be together that much," he said, sounding as if he were preoccupied. "The arrangement we have is a trial—remember that. As much as we can, we'll live together under the same roof when you're not performing, and for now you'll call the ranch home. As soon as possible, we'll all go to the ranch."

"That will be a totally new experience for me and my sisters. Noah won't know the difference," she said, enjoying dancing with Marek as she always did. He looked incredibly handsome, and for a fleeting second she wished life had been different. The longing was gone as swiftly as it had come.

"You can get whatever decorator you want," Marek said. "We've already made changes at our Dallas house."

"*Our* house—it will take a while to become accustomed to thinking that way. I'm still astounded at how fast you got the changes in I wanted."

"It's our house from this day forward, until we make a legal change."

"That sounds permanent. The ranch is another thing I'm trying to become accustomed to. Horses, cattle, ranches—I know nothing about them."

"Ranch life is pretty plain. It's hard work, but just taking care of cattle, horses, land, fences, a million things strung out over lots of land. It won't mean much to you, and when you're there, you won't even know it's going on."

"My ring is beautiful. Thank you again."

"I'm glad you like it. Let's get through this and out of here when we can. I'm ready to be alone with you. You look gorgeous today."

"Thank you," she said, smiling at him. "You're nice. You look supremely handsome."

He smiled. "Mutual admiration. That's good. There's so much that's good. I'm happy, Camille."

They circled the dance floor in silence.

"I like dancing with you, but we can do that on our honeymoon," Marek said finally. "After this dance, we probably should circulate and talk to guests so we can get out of here sooner. I want you to myself," he repeated.

"Marek, just a reminder, I can't rush into anything physical."

"We've agreed on that subject, and I promised it would be mutual." He leaned close to her ear. "I'll tell you now. I'm going to seduce you, Camille. I want to make love to you. You're a desirable woman," he whispered, making her tingle, although she suspected he was trying to smooth over the lack of deep feelings between them.

"I could be a little green woman from Mars and you wouldn't notice," she said.

"Not true. I know I'm with a beautiful, desirable woman," he said in a warm voice, looking down at her in one of the rare moments when it seemed as if he really saw her as a woman.

The ballad ended and another began. Her father appeared to ask her to dance, and Marek left to ask his mother.

By early afternoon she saw Marek give her a look and then glance toward the door. She sat at a table with her family. "I think we're leaving now," she said. She gave each one a hug and stopped longer with Ashley. Noah had fallen asleep beside her in his carrier. "Don't hesitate to text about anything. Keep in touch."

"You'll hear from me often. Don't worry. He'll be fine. We'll all take care of him."

"Take care, Ashley, and call if there's anything. Marek can have us flown right back here."

"I know he can. See you in a few days. Enjoy the water and palm trees. And your handsome husband."

Camille laughed and hugged her sister briefly. "I will."

Joining her, Marek took her hand to rush to the waiting limo that took them to the airport and a Rangel plane.

As they headed east over Texas, Marek gazed out the window. Noah would be part of his life now. He already had an attorney working on the adoption. In spite of wanting this marriage and being overjoyed that Camille had accepted, he had hurt earlier today. The morning had distressed him, bringing back too many memories of Jillian.

The marriage ceremony had opened old wounds. Camille had been aware of his pain. Her kindness and understanding and, later, her happy expectations and quiet cheer, had lifted him out of the hurt. She was a beautiful, intelligent, talented woman. For that afternoon, at least, he had forgotten and set aside the past, something that was happening more and more since she had come into his life. Now he reached out to take her hand, then impulsively tugged her closer and leaned forward to kiss her. It was a brief kiss because anything longer would set him on fire.

When he sat back, he smiled at her, and she smiled in return. "It's been a good day," she said. He nodded.

She had been convincing in assuring him that a marriage of convenience was all right. He knew people who felt that way and then fell in love and marriage was the thing they wanted most. She had made her choices, and both Camille and her family seemed happy.

Their wedding night would be a letdown for most, but they had had a frank talk about their plans for this honeymoon and both had agreed to set aside a physical relationship at this point in their lives. He would let their relationship develop at whatever pace worked out, but he wanted to make love to her. It would please him if they could have a real wedding night.

He thought about the day's events. His parents had seemed wary of Camille and Noah. They always had great interest in Ginny's girls when they were with them. Once they returned to California, they seemed to retreat back into their own world. Perhaps they'd come around to welcoming Camille and Noah.

Shifting his attention to Camille again, he wished her long hair was down. She looked sophisticated, composed, satisfied. Her expression and demeanor hid the stormy emotions he was sure she battled.

"You look beautiful. You have all day," he said, meaning what he told her.

"Thank you. And you look breathtakingly handsome in your new tux and your fancy new boots."

He wiggled his foot. "Thank you. I don't know about fancy, but they are new, clean and comfortable."

"The boots made the men in the wedding look like the cowboys they are."

"Frank didn't have on boots. Just Jess and I did. My dad wore them. He's continued wearing them even after leaving the ranch."

"I'm excited about our destination. I know this may be old to you, but it's a marvel I haven't experienced before."

"Enjoy yourself. Just don't swim alone except in our pool."

"*Our* pool. You've made the transition quickly."

"I'm trying to. This is what I wanted and I'll go as far

as I can to make it work. In every way, Camille," he added, thinking about the physical side. Her cheeks flushed, so he knew she understood his reference and reacted to it.

She turned to look outside, and he glanced down at the band on his finger. It seemed unreal in so many ways. Marek touched the band, which was wide and plain gold. Jillian's face floated in front of him, her cascade of white-blond hair, her large blue-green eyes, her smile that always made him smile in return. He took a deep breath. He missed her so and she was supposed to be sitting beside him as he headed off for his honeymoon. Instead, he was traveling with a black-haired beauty he barely knew.

"You're thinking about Jillian, aren't you?" Camille asked gently, touching his hand.

"Yes. It's the wedding that's triggered a lot of memories. They'll fade out of my thoughts. Sorry."

"Don't be ridiculous," she said. "I understand."

"I'm surprised, because you've never lost anyone extremely close."

She shook her head. "No, but I've played characters who have, and I have given a lot of thought to feelings and reactions."

"Maybe that's part of your success," he said, speculating about her and realizing he should hear her perform. "I wonder if Noah will sing. Kern could whistle. That was his musical ability." He grinned. "My brother didn't sing. If he did, the dogs started howling."

She laughed, and his insides heated. She was not only beautiful, but desirable. Her laughter was an enticing, contagious sound.

"You should have had more laughter today," he said.

"I'm doing all right. I never thought about Noah singing. Right now, I think more about him talking. Do you think your family will ever accept Noah or me?" she asked.

"If we stay together, probably more than they do now. They've surprised me. I didn't expect the reaction I got from them at all. Frankly, I think my mother is afraid to let go and love him. She loved Kern. When we were growing up, I always thought she favored him. Ginny and I both did. Kern was probably more lovable than we were. He could charm anyone. I think she's scared of getting hurt again if she gets too close to Noah. If she lets go and loves him, she wouldn't want to go back to California. My dad could be feeling the same. Don't let it worry you. They'll go back to California before we return and you won't see them for a long time."

"I'm just sorry they didn't welcome Noah. He's a sweetheart. They know you did a paternity test, don't they?"

"Yes, they do," Marek said, unable to understand how his parents could so easily reject Kern's baby when they knew he was their grandson. "Don't worry about it. They shouldn't be that important to you. I think they tried to avoid seeing Noah, just so they wouldn't become attached. We'll be together sometime when Ginny's girls are around and they'll have to get to know him. If they do, I expect them to change. How can they resist him?"

She smiled. "I quite agree. He's the most adorable baby in the whole world," she said, and Marek smiled with her. "Ahh, I made you smile. That's good. A real smile." She patted his hand, a light, warm touch that heightened his awareness of her.

"Well, at least my family has accepted you. Actually, they're grateful for all you've done for us."

Marek reached over to take a pin out of her hair. "I like your hair down. The wedding is over and it's just us."

She smiled at him as her long, raven locks fell.

"Giving away money is the easiest part of this. Making the changes in our lives—that's the hard part. You can't always predict the outcome of your actions," he said, concentrating on taking down her hair. When it fell freely, she shook her head. His pulse quickened. The midnight cascade fell over her shoulders, framing her face and giving her a more earthy appearance. With her lush curves and flowing hair, she looked hot-blooded and passionate. He could remember kissing her in total detail because it had been a sizzling kiss.

"Were you and Kern always close?"

"Yes. He just tagged along after me and I accepted that. Sometimes I thought he was a pest and would shake him, but most of the time I let him come with me or do what I was doing. By the time we were out of high school, we were becoming close, a closeness that grew as we did things together. As adults, the age difference didn't matter. I miss him every day. I could count on him for a lot."

"That's sort of a description of my relationship with Ashley. Not so much Stephanie, who is older. A lot of the time she did her own thing. She has a deep regard for money, so you couldn't have picked a better way to win her over."

"Works with most people," he replied, even though he knew it was a cynical attitude.

"If I hadn't thought this would be good for Noah, I wouldn't have agreed for any amount," she said quietly, and he gazed into her blue eyes that held him as if she had immobilized him.

"I don't think you would have," he replied and they lapsed into silence.

"I can't wait to get there."

"We'll get there in time for a swim, and then we can have a long, leisurely dinner overlooking the water. And there are palm trees around the veranda. I made sure of that before I leased this place."

She smiled. "I want to wish the plane there now. It sounds like paradise."

He didn't want to point out that paradise would be doing

this with a person she loved. She seemed happy, and he wasn't trying to shoot down her joy because it was a difficult situation. A strained honeymoon with a stranger, both of them locked into a paper marriage of convenience. He had never expected to find himself in any such thing. And he would not have been if Jillian had lived. He would have been married to her by now, perhaps starting his own family, and he would have had to let Noah go and only see the child from time to time. Taking a deep breath, he dropped his thoughts of Jillian and any "what-ifs." With Camille to keep his mind elsewhere, he was finding it easier to focus on the present, and that's what he needed to do—try to be the best husband and dad he could be.

When they finally flew over the Caribbean, Camille hovered by the window, fascinated as a child by the bright blue water below. "Marek, it's beautiful! It's what I've imagined."

"Camille, you've been south and have seen sights like this—Houston, San Diego, Miami."

"Only Houston—I haven't gone to Galveston or along the coast. I've been on northern coasts and in Europe, but I haven't been to Miami or San Diego."

"I'm surprised." He smiled slightly again, watching her turn back to look, glad she was enjoying herself because he thought this so-called honeymoon in Grand Cayman was cheating her in too many ways.

They landed, and all her attention was on their surroundings as they drove to the villa he had leased. It was within high walls with a gatekeeper. The security wasn't obvious, but Marek had already hired a company and knew it was in place. When they stepped out of the limo he took her hand to go inside.

"I love this," she said, inhaling deeply, her gaze roaming over the sprawling villa. "I see we'll have security here."

"We will and a full staff who will stay out of our way.

Under the circumstances I didn't see any point in dismissing the staff," he remarked.

"This is a magic place and maybe magic will happen."

"You've been performing in make-believe stories too long," he said, still amused by her enthusiasm. "Don't count on magic. I know you have been places far more exotic and beautiful than this."

"It's what captures your fancy that becomes so special. And this does mine more than castles and mountains and bustling cities."

He swept her into his arms, and her eyes flew wide. For the first time since they had flown away from the U.S., he had her full attention. "I'll follow an old tradition even though it's ridiculous for us. This may be the only marriage for either one of us, so I intend to do what I can to make it work and to keep you happy."

She smiled broadly and wrapped her arms around his neck, her blue eyes ensnaring him in that manner she had. "Watch out, my husband, or you'll cause me to fall in love with you. Neither of us can cope with that."

"I don't think there's much danger, but if you do, we're married."

"If I do, then I will do everything in my power to make you fall in love with me," she whispered, suddenly looking solemn. "That's a promise," she said, tapping his chest with her forefinger while he carried her over the threshold and inside.

He looked at her intently, desire stirring as it had the night he had kissed her. It had surprised him then and it did now. With their gazes locked, he set her on her feet. She still had her arms around his neck and she gazed up at him, fires in the depths of blue, a sultry invitation that made his heart beat faster.

He forgot the past and was lost in the moment. His gaze

lowered to her mouth and he remembered her steamy kiss, a kiss that had jolted him and pulled him solidly into the present. He leaned down, placing his lips on hers while her arm tightened around his neck.

She pressed her soft curves against him. She was tall, warm and enticing. The moment his mouth touched hers, thoughts shut down, desire flickered to life. He tightened his arm around her narrow waist, pulling her closer against him. Long-dormant feelings stirred. His body came to life, heart pounding, fire consuming him while she kissed him passionately in return.

Her kisses were fiery and demanding. That energy and zest for life that she exhibited channeled into passion and melted him. His body responded fully. Desire rocked him. She surprised him when she leaned away. "Marek, wait," she gasped. "Let's not complicate our lives more. I'm not ready for a purely physical relationship in spite of saying marriage vows today. We've both agreed on that."

Raising his head, he tried to get his breath. His body needed to cool. He desired her and suspected it would take little to crumble her argument and seduce her.

"I want to wait, and our kisses are leading to lovemaking," she added. "This isn't what either of us planned."

Six

Camille tried to catch her breath. Her heart pounded, and every nerve was alive. She wanted Marek, but she had meant her argument. What she hadn't told him was that she was not going to fall into his arms and into his bed at the first few kisses because it would be totally meaningless to him.

Sooner or later he would overcome his grief and he would want her physically, but it was lust and nothing else. If she succumbed, it was not going to be the first afternoon they were husband and wife, when they had nothing between them except working out this paper marriage and Noah's care.

She intended to stick to what she had said, even though her body clamored for more. She wanted his kisses, wanted his lovemaking, but common sense said at this point that was the road to disaster. If she went to bed with him, she wanted him to be aware of her as a desirable woman, to remember she was his wife, to truly want her and know her way better than he did at the moment.

His brown eyes had darkened to midnight, and he was breathing heavily. He looked as if he could devour her. She didn't know whether he was weighing her argument or trying to get desire under control as he stood staring at her.

Walking away from him, she viewed the open living area in front of her.

"This is fantastic," she declared, trying to focus on something besides Marek and her own desire for more kisses. "It's perfect and more than I dreamed." The entrance opened into an airy, large living area with columns dividing the room from an adjoining dining area. Floor-to-ceiling glass doors opened to a veranda that ran the length of the house. Beyond it was the pool with fountains and gardens that overlooked the white beach and clear blue water. Tall palms ran along one side of the veranda, and there were palms scattered between the white beach and the water.

Camille walked outside, inhaling deeply and holding out her arms. "It's gorgeous." She spun around to tell him. He stood only a few feet behind her, watching her with such cool speculation in his eyes that her pulse jumped. Was he thinking about their marriage and what it might mean?

"This is perfect, Marek. I'm so happy with it. I won't want to leave."

"Yes, you will. You'll miss Noah. You'll feel guilty about missing your voice practice and language studies."

"I plan to do those here."

"Because of Noah, you'll be ready to leave, but I'm glad you like it. For now we can change and swim or we can just sit out here, have drinks and then dinner."

"A swim. I have to get into that water. I'll beat you there," she said, rushing past him, and he smiled again.

He was ready first, waiting when she came out. She wore a pink T-shirt that came to mid-thigh and hid her curves. She was aware of his scrutiny, far more aware of him. He wore plaid trunks. His muscled chest was bare; his broad shoulders and arms were hard muscles, probably from the ranch work he did. He had a smattering of dark chest curls and his legs were long. Realizing she was staring, she dropped her things and pulled off her T-shirt, hotly aware that he watched her.

She turned, flipping her head, causing her hair to swing back over her shoulders.

"I'll race you in," she said, dashing past him. In seconds he passed her and ran in the water ahead of her, splashing out until it was deep enough to swim. After a few strokes he turned to watch her as she caught up.

"You're a good swimmer," he said.

"You're better. You beat me."

"I used to compete in swimming a long time ago."

"Then I won't challenge you again."

"You challenge me on a regular basis," he said in a husky voice. He was flirting with her. A subtle change in their relationship.

"I didn't think you noticed."

"I'm not completely numb."

"Did you say 'numb' or 'dumb'?" she asked sweetly, teasing him. He laughed and splashed her with a wave of water. She shrieked and swam away. In a flash he caught up and swam beside her. He grasped her upper arm lightly while he treaded water.

"See that buoy?" he said, pointing at an orange buoy that bobbed gently in the small waves. "They told me that is the farthest out we should swim. It's much deeper and tides are stronger."

Glancing back at the beach, she was surprised how far they had come. "This water is beautiful."

"It's prettier when you snorkel. I have all-new equipment on the beach."

"Then, Mr. Expert Swimmer, I'll race you back to it," she

said, starting to swim as vigorously as possible. For a few seconds, he let her lead and then he passed her. When she walked out of the water, he waited, and she could feel his gaze drifting slowly over her in a long, leisurely look that became almost a caress. She tingled from head to toe. Desire ignited, a flame deep inside. Her awareness heightened of the skimpiness of her two-piece red suit.

"Where's the snorkel equipment?"

"Maybe we should just stay out here and enjoy the scenery," he drawled, still studying her.

"I think that's the way to complications. We discussed this earlier," she said without moving. She tried to keep her gaze on his face, to keep from looking him over as he was her. He was breathtaking, masculine, sexy.

"Marek, where did you put the equipment?"

"Camille, the best equipment on this beach is what I'm looking at," he said, walking to her. "You're gorgeous. I can't stop looking," he added.

"Yes, you can," she said, her words sounding distant to her. "Snorkel equipment or I go inside and dress."

He walked up to place his hands on her shoulders and she was riveted, her threat of leaving impossible to carry out. His light touch burned as if it had been a brand. Aware of him only inches away, she tingled. Could he hear her pounding heart?

His arm slipped around her waist. "You're bringing me back to life. I didn't think it was possible."

"For that, I'm glad," she said, meaning it, but barely able to focus on conversation. His hands were on her, his body only inches away and both of them wore very little. All her cool reserve had shattered, and the look in his eyes was something new in their relationship, yet age-old, blatantly sexy. She was breathless, too aware of his body, his arm around her and his mouth so close. She looked up into dark eyes with fire in their depths.

"For the first time in over a year I feel alive," he whispered. He drew her closer and leaned down to kiss her. His mouth was on hers, his tongue stroking her with slow deliberation that made her pounding heart race.

She slid her hands over his smooth back, pressed against him and felt his arousal. Her arms tightened as she returned his kiss eagerly, unable to resist, knowing they both had just crossed a line.

There would be no going back from this fiery kiss to an occasional peck on the cheek. She closed her eyes tightly, relishing the feel of his hard muscles, his strength, the deepening passion in his kisses.

His hands ran over her back and bottom, down along her bare thighs.

She finally ended the kisses. "Slow down, Marek. This changes everything far too fast. Let's cool down before our lives take another turn and complications beset us."

Breathing hard, he gazed at her with longing in his expression. With a pounding heart, she tried to cling to the sensible speech she had just made, but that wasn't what her heart wanted. She stepped back. "We should swim," she whispered. She passed him, heading to the water to cool down and to put some distance between them. Their lives had just taken another major turn. Was it already out of her control?

He showed her how to wear her goggles. His casual touches were even more disturbing than before. She had always had a reaction to him, but not as intense as it had now become. Desire was a constant, a hot, running need that she hoped to control.

In minutes, the fascinating sea creatures swimming around her captured her attention. Finally, Marek tugged on her arm and motioned to get out.

As they surfaced, she took off the breathing tube. Marek was beside her. Tall, muscular, appealing—how could she return to being casual, unaffected? Close to shore, they could easily stand in water that was only a little over four feet deep.

"It's later than you think. Let's have a drink and then dinner so I can release the staff for this evening."

"Certainly. That was fascinating. I want to come back in the morning," she said, thinking Marek was far more fascinating.

He looked amused. "You can snorkel all day if you'd like. The fish won't mind."

"When was the first time you came here?"

"I've never been to this particular villa, but the Caymans, probably when I was five or six. I don't even remember."

"You've done it all. No wonder nothing excites you."

"Oh, yes, there are things that excite me," he replied, his voice changing as he flirted again.

"I'm not asking what."

"Who, not what. You already know the answer."

Pulling on her T-shirt, she wriggled it down over her hips, glancing around to see him watching her.

She picked up all her things. "I'll change and be back."

"Sure," he said, flipping a towel over his shoulder as he headed inside with her.

After a shower, she dressed in a deep blue cotton sundress and sandals and dried her hair, letting it fall loosely over her shoulders. When she went outside, he was waiting at the table. He looked relaxed in chinos and a navy knit shirt. A chilled bottle of champagne was on ice and he had already partially filled two flutes. He handed one to her and picked up the other.

"Here's to a happy union that blesses all concerned, especially Noah."

"I'll drink to that," she said, touching his glass lightly,

watching bubbles rise in the pale golden champagne. She sipped her drink and looked out to sea.

"Sit here, Camille. We'll have our drinks before dinner."

She sat in a lawn chair, and he sat in another close beside her. "This is truly beautiful, Marek, and I'm having a wonderful time."

"I'm glad," he said, gazing at the water. She was beginning to be able to tell when he was thinking of his fiancée and grief was present because his voice and expression were both remote.

"This is the hardest time of day. Sundown. Somehow it seems a time of loss. The sunshine is gone, the night isn't here. This is when I've had a bad time. You'd think it would be late at night, which sometimes it is, but this time of day really gets me." He talked, but she thought he had almost forgotten her. He was looking toward the horizon. To the west the sun was a ball of orange fire only half-visible above the horizon.

She couldn't think of anything to say that would help him. He was wrapped in his own world, and his hurt was understandable, but at least today, he had had moments when his pain had lifted and she had glimpsed the lively man he was before the crash.

She gazed out to sea, still shocked that she was locked into a marriage of convenience with a man who might always love another woman. Would he break her heart if she fell in love with him? She would do exactly as her father had suggested—keep the money tucked away so she could return it if this arrangement did not work out to everyone's satisfaction.

"Marek, what do you want from life? You've already been enormously successful in business. You have the ranch you love."

"I want to be a dad for Noah. I hope our marriage and this arrangement work out."

"Aside from Noah, what do you hope to achieve? You have an enormous fortune, so it's not that. What is it?"

"Still make money. Also to help others. I have certain charities and, of those, there are a few I'm particularly interested in. I've established a ranch for homeless kids. It's not far out of Fort Worth. Some kids are there on a temporary basis, some permanent. I've gone through our church."

"That's great," she said, surprised by his answer.

"Don't sound so startled that I would help someone."

"I'm just surprised at the particular project."

"I only put up the money and helped them get established, but I've liked working with them occasionally. For my own pleasure I've done calf roping in rodeos this past year—and won, amazingly enough. That takes my mind off everything else. Do you like rodeos?"

"I know as much about them as you do opera."

"Maybe a rodeo is like an opera—you either love it or you don't like it at all."

Smiling, she shook her head. "Rodeos and opera—I don't think you can quite lump them together even in that way."

"I'll take you to a rodeo sometime soon. There'll be one in New Mexico."

They talked, drifting from one subject to another until dinner was served, delicious blackened grouper.

Over dinner, conversation became more impersonal and she felt better about him. The staff was discreet, keeping out of sight most of the time.

After dinner the dishes were cleared away while they moved to another area on the veranda. Marek spoke briefly to the staff and then joined her again. It was almost dark, and various veranda lights and torches on the beach had come on or been lighted.

"I suppose Jess runs the ranch when you're not there."

"Jess runs the ranch when I'm there and when I'm not there."

"He's sort of closed off from the world. Or maybe just quiet. Is he married?"

"No. Jess is closed off from the world to a degree. Jess had a wife and son. They were killed in a car wreck years ago. If anyone understands what I've felt, it's Jess. He never married again. He has a solitary life, but he gets along. We understand each other, and I can count on him."

"That's dreadful. Both of you with such similar losses."

"He's never had to say anything. He's just been there for me, which helped. After the plane crash sometimes he'd come up to the house in the evening and bring cold beer. We'd sit, drink and maybe not say three words all evening, just sit on the porch and sip beer. It helped just to know he understood and he was there."

"I'm glad you had somebody."

"Jess is all for this marriage and bringing Noah into our lives."

"You just never know what problems other people carry around," she said quietly. "I've been fortunate."

"When we get back, we'll get your things, Ashley's and Noah's moved to the ranch."

"Noah growing up a little cowboy—that seems impossible."

"It's possible. I'll get a horse for you. You can ride with me early in the mornings if you'd like. This time of year it's beautiful out."

She laughed. "I don't know one thing about horses, but I would love to learn. That sounds fun, Marek."

"Life's a blast for you, isn't it?"

"A lot of the time. It's a lot of work and sometimes scary, too."

Finally, she said she would turn in.

"Before you do, let's walk on the beach. The moon is out and I think you'll like a stroll. You can't do that at home."

With his arm draped casually across her shoulders, they walked along the sandy beach, where flickering torches cast yellow-and-orange reflections over the dark waters and high-lighted whitecaps. When he walked with her to her bedroom door, she turned to face him.

"This is a weird wedding night, Camille. You're getting shortchanged here."

"No, I'm not. I'm getting a lot from this marriage. I expect a lot."

One dark eyebrow arched. "How's that? Don't expect me to fall in love. I'm coming out of my grief, I'll admit, but I'll never be in—" She placed her finger on his mouth.

"That wasn't what I was talking about, but that, too. You don't know what lies ahead. I expect you to be a father for Noah. A good father. You've given us a fortune. Because of this marriage, I'm wealthy and my family has options and can do things they could not have done otherwise."

"You see the world through rose-colored glasses."

"Maybe, but that makes for a pretty world," she said, smiling at him. She stood on tiptoe, wrapped her arm around his neck and kissed him on the mouth. She wanted to shake him out of his insulated world. Marek's arm circled her waist and he returned her kiss, holding her tightly while he wound his other hand in her hair. Her pulse roared in her ears and her heartbeat raced as she kissed him, pouring herself into the kiss, wanting to break through the barriers around his heart. She had started the kiss, but then Marek dominated, burning away caution, causing wild responses from her.

When he picked her up to carry her into her bedroom, she realized they were headed for a real wedding night. "Wait, Marek—" she whispered.

"You started this," he said in a voice that was as deep as

a growl. Giving her a searching look, he set her on her feet. Her heart pounded, part desire, part exhilaration that she had shaken him out of his remote numbness as she had intended.

"We stop now," she said. "Weird wedding night or not, it's been more than either of us expected. Far more than I ever expected. I still don't want to rush complications."

"I think complications are barreling down on us," he said. "You have to take some of the blame. You're filled with a zest for life that's irresistible. I believe you started this tonight."

"I don't have any regrets," she whispered and saw a flicker in the depths of his dark eyes. "I've had a wonderful wedding day. It's not what either of us would have if we could have whatever we want, but under the circumstances, for a paper marriage, it was a great day."

"I agree. I wondered how I would get through it. Thanks. You got me through this one and it's been good."

"Will you be all right tonight?"

"I don't know," he replied. "Want to come hold my hand and make sure I am?" he replied, a faint smile hovering on his mouth.

She laughed. "Good try, but not this night. You'll be okay. Let's have a sunrise swim."

"Sure. Want me to come get you out of bed?"

"Another good try, but, no, I don't. I'll be up early. And I'm sure, as a rancher, you get up early every morning. If not, I'll go on without you."

"And me miss the sight of you in your swimsuit? I think not. I'll be there."

She laughed. "Good night, Marek." He caught her up, holding her tightly to kiss her hard. Just as abruptly he released her.

"Some night, Camille, you won't tell me to wait."

"Just make sure that's what you want," she whispered as her heart raced.

"I can give you the same warning." He left, closing the door behind him.

Staring at the door, she gave herself over to memories of the whole evening. Whether it would complicate her life horribly or not, she was going to fall in love with her husband. Or maybe she was already in love with him.

When she was ready for bed, she stepped onto the veranda outside her bedroom. Moonlight spilled across the water in one long, white beam. She was married to a Rangel now. Mrs. Marek Rangel. This was never how she had dreamed she would have her wedding night. It could have been different tonight. Was she ready for that big a change?

"It will work out," she told herself, thinking how Marek seemed now compared to the day she had walked into his office. She thought about their kisses, escalating in intensity. She combed her hair back from her face with her fingers, thinking about being in Marek's arms today, dancing with him, the moment he had swept her up to carry her over the threshold. Just when she thought she had him figured out, he surprised her. She finally fell asleep in a chair, dozing and then waking to crawl into bed to sleep.

The next two days they spent swimming, eating, dancing and getting to know each other better, yet all the while, she felt sparks and tension growing between them.

The last night they went into town to a show and afterward they went to a popular bar. The steamy bar was raucous, the dancing frenzied, strobe lights flashing. Marek unbuttoned his short-sleeve island shirt, letting go after the past month filled with tension and a strained wedding filled with painful memories.

Relaxed, he enjoyed dancing. Afterward, when the floor was cleared for limbo, they watched as a few patrons tried it. The crowd got into it, cheering on the dancers.

Marek had his arm around her shoulder, but he stepped

out to participate. The music was deafening, and he concentrated on trying to get down. After the first easy try, they lowered the bar. Again, he made it to cheers and clapping. He grinned at Camille. They lowered the bar and he tried once again to louder cheers. He laughed as Camille gave him a thumbs-up.

Feeling sweat pour off himself, he motioned for another try, getting lower than any of the amateurs so far until he felt his balance going. He put down his hand to wiggle under the bar and bounced to his feet to cheers and applause as he bowed.

Laughing, he caught her around her waist.

"I didn't know you were so talented," she yelled over the noise of the crowd. He led her back to the bar and the bartender gave him a cold beer and congratulations.

"Hey, man, beer's on the house," he said, grinning.

As Marek took a long drink, Camille laughed. They walked back into the crowd to watch the dancers until the professional dancer returned to outdo everyone else.

When they stopped the limbo, a samba began, and Marek took her hand to dance. He already knew she was an excellent dancer. As she followed his moves across the dance floor, he realized they were in perfect step. Her red dress with a halter top had a skirt that was fitted over her hips and then flared fully below. With every turn her legs were revealed, drawing an audience quickly.

With his gaze locked with hers they danced in unison as if they had practiced for weeks. The fast, sexy dance sent his heart racing. Every move felt even more exhilarating. He watched her twist her hips while dancing in perfect step with him. She was taunting and sexy, and he wanted her. Desire burned hotly, more than the scorching air in the bar. He wished he had her alone, far away from a crowd.

The growing audience began to circle and watch, cheering them on, whistling and clapping until the end when they got resounding cheers. Exhilarated, filled with energy, he laughed as he pulled her to him. "Let's give them a thrill," he said and kissed her, dipping with her so she had to put her arms around his neck. Dimly, above his roaring pulse, he heard the crowd go wild with yells.

Wanting to take her home and to bed now, he swung her up to audience applause. "Take your bow. You're a great dancer. How you did that and stayed as cool as you look, I don't know." They bowed and walked away while the band took a break. Marek wiped his sweat-covered forehead and pushed back tangled locks of his black hair.

Camille caught her long hair to braid it swiftly. "I need a clip or rubber band for this hair."

He took her hand and they crossed to the bar to get one. As soon as she fastened her braid, he held her arm and they went outside, where welcome cool air hit her. He spun her around. Her eyes widened and she placed her hands against his chest.

While Camille's heart pounded, he pulled her to him to kiss her possessively. She wrapped her arms around him to kiss him in return. His body was hot, damp from the dance, flat planes and hard muscles. His hand ran down her back and over her bottom and she was thankful they were at the bar and not at the villa with privacy and bedrooms. She still didn't want to get into an intimate relationship and complicate their lives and do something that he would take as lightly as he had the dancing tonight.

His kisses stirred passion to a storm that buffeted her. In spite of her caution, she wanted him. She ran her hands over his back, wanting to tug his shirt out of his chinos but resisting.

His tongue went deep, a demanding kiss that shook her.

He was not steeped in grief tonight. Far from it. He had been losing the past swiftly, and tonight his body was hot with desire.

Relishing their kisses, she didn't want to stop, either, aware their location would eventually end their lovemaking before it went too far. Momentarily letting go of her caution, she kissed him eagerly, sliding her hands over his chest to feel the solid muscles. He was aroused, sexy. Knowing she shouldn't, she couldn't keep from wanting him. In spite of knowing he was a threat to her career, she wanted him, but she wanted more of him than just his body. Even when she shouldn't, she wanted his heart.

His hand went to her throat and then slipped lower, over her breast, and she gasped with pleasure as he caressed her. She closed her hand around his wrist.

"Marek, we're in a very public place."

"There's no one paying any attention to us. They're all inside. You're a fabulous dancer," he replied in a muffled voice as he continued to shower kisses on her throat, moving lower. He shoved the neck of her dress lower to kiss her. She wriggled and stepped back, straightening her dress.

"We can go back and dance or go to the villa, but we need to stop the lovemaking out here in public."

He gave her a long steady look before he finally nodded. "Which is it? What do you want to do? Dance more or go back?"

"Go back and walk on the beach. It's our last night."

"The last night of our honeymoon. We could make it real, Camille," he said in a husky voice.

"You mean we could make love. It would not be real love between us, and you know that. You said you didn't mind having a relationship without sex for now."

"I didn't think I wanted one. You're making me want things I didn't think I would. This past week—maybe even before—for the first time since I lost Jillian and Kern, I feel like life is good again."

"Frankly, I'm glad. I want some kind of caring between us if we have a physical relationship. You agreed to that."

"So I did," he said. "We'll have some kind of caring, Camille. I already do care," he said, his dark eyes holding her spellbound. He leaned close to kiss her, his mouth firm, demanding on hers until three men burst outside, noisily spilling past them.

Marek leaned away and smiled at her. "All right, we'll go back to the villa. I'll get the car," he said, sending a text message.

"It was fun to dance. We did well together," she said when he finished sending the text.

"Amazingly well. I'll bet people who watched thought we had danced a samba together dozens of times. Frankly, it surprised me."

"I had years of dance lessons when I was growing up. Someday we'll come back maybe and try and see if it happens again."

"That sounds good—someday we'll come back. This is a good marriage."

"I think you've had too much to drink tonight."

He shook his head. "Hardly. I had two beers all evening long. I didn't finish the last one, so it wasn't even two. For a paper marriage it's a good marriage."

"There. That description is far more accurate. Let's go."

As soon as they reached the villa, they went outside for the walk along the beach that she had wanted. Kicking off her shoes, she listened to waves lap against the shore.

"I've finally cooled off. The bar was hot, dancing even hotter," she said.

"Kissing you was the hottest of all," he added, and she smiled.

"I could have added that but didn't. This has been wonderful. Thank you for finding this place and the villa—it has fulfilled a dream I've had for a long time."

"I'm glad you're pleased. I'm glad you're here for the first time with me. Tomorrow we'll return home, and next week we'll go to the ranch and plan the changes you want to make."

"I need to get back the following week. It's getting closer to performance time, and I have to practice. My time will be more deeply involved with my profession."

"I understand. I may stay at the ranch some of the time and keep out of your way."

She nodded, wondering how well they would work out their time and if he would accept the demands of her career. She suspected he was unaccustomed to having to give up anything he wanted in daily living.

"Stephanie is not interested in ranch life. Right now, she's delighted to be going back to Saint Louis. I think she'll open an office and work from there. She'll do my accounting, but I'm going to hire another manager because she wants to go home and settle down. Remember, Ashley is going to Saint Louis for the week when we return to Dallas. They'll both be gone and I'll take care of Noah."

"That's when you'll need to let me or Ginny help take care of him."

"At this point, I feel better about Ginny. She's accustomed to caring for a baby. You're not."

He smiled, and her heartbeat quickened. Her response to him was increasing instead of diminishing with familiarity.

After they walked along the beach, they sat on the veranda, sipping iced tea and talking until she realized the time. "Do you know how early we've planned to leave? It's three in the morning."

"With a phone call I can change tomorrow's flight."

Thinking about the week ahead, she shook her head. "We

should get back. We have plans made and everyone will be expecting us."

They walked to her bedroom door, where they stopped as they had each night. "It's been good, Marek," she said, aware of his disheveled state, his shirt unbuttoned, revealing his muscled chest, his tangled hair falling partially on his forehead. His shirttail was out of his chinos. He looked sexy, ready for love.

"Thanks to you, this trip has been a good one. Tonight was a blast and a relief to just let go in every way."

She smiled at him. "I'm glad. Good night," she said, reaching up to put her hand on his shoulder and kiss him lightly. The kiss changed into a passionate one that had them both gasping for breath when they stopped.

"Sometime, Camille, you won't say no."

"I imagine you're right," she whispered. She stepped into her room and closed the door, her heart pounding. "I didn't want to tonight," she whispered, touching her tingling lips lightly with the back of her fingers. She looked at the ring on her hand, watching the diamond sparkle. "Mrs. Marek Rangel. I want it all. I want your love, and then this ring will hold meaning," she whispered, wondering whether he could ever let go and love again. She mulled over his remark earlier—*I already do care.* How much did he care? Tiny changes had happened, and maybe they were making a difference in him. Would he ever fall in love or forever be holding a memory in his heart?

And what if he did fall in love? Would she wreck her life and the career she had guarded and given all her effort to for her lifetime? She couldn't imagine living in isolation on his ranch. Voice and language lessons would be an impossibility. If he ever fell in love, was she willing to sacrifice what she had achieved?

Seven

The trip to Dallas seemed short, and she felt a rush of joy as Noah held out his arms and kicked his legs at the sight of her. She scooped him up to hug him, looking over his head at Ashley, who smiled happily.

Marek stood beside her and she handed Noah to him. "Thank you, Ashley."

"Ma-ma," Noah said. Startled, Camille looked at him and then at Ashley, who laughed and shrugged.

"He's beginning to talk. He has a two-word vocabulary— ma-ma and bah for bottle."

"I missed his first word," Camille said, shaking her head.

"I did videotape it for you. I wanted to surprise you when you returned and heard him. Also, I'm going shortly if that's all right with you," Ashley replied. "I'll stay with my friend Patty Collins tonight and be back early because I'm going to Saint Louis tomorrow."

"Of course, run along. We're fine, and we'll see you in the morning."

"Great to have you back," she said. "I'll see you later, Camille. Bye, Marek."

"Goodbye, Ashley," he replied, making noises at Noah that made the baby laugh.

Sitting on the floor, Marek played with Noah while Camille left to unpack. Later, she showered and changed to blue shorts and a T-shirt. She returned to find Marek holding Noah in a rocking chair and reading a story to him.

"He doesn't know a word you're saying," she said, laughing.

"Look at him. He likes this. He's happy and listening."

"He must be on the verge of falling asleep."

"You just can't admit that he's precocious and likes being read to."

"No, I can't," she said. "And neither can you. Try that in the morning when he gets up."

Noah wiggled and hit the book with his hand. "See," Marek said, glancing at her. "He wants me to read."

"You just go ahead and read. When you're ready, I'll put him in bed."

Marek read softly to Noah without bothering to answer her. She stared at them, amazed Noah would sit still as if he were hanging on each word.

Marek turned a page. "I just have the magic touch."

She laughed and shook her head. "What you have is an exhausted baby. I'll bet he's asleep in ten minutes."

"Bet a few kisses and I'll take you up on it."

"I'll win. What do I get if I win?" she asked, placing her hand on her hip to wait.

"What do you want?" he asked.

She tilted her head. "Live dangerously—be surprised. I'll tell you when I win."

"Deal," he replied, his gaze raking over her before he returned to reading. Glancing at her watch to make note of the time, she left to write thank-you notes for wedding gifts. It astounded her how fast Marek had rooms remodeled and changes made. She had come by often to look at the progress or answer questions, but they had the house ready and the move was made three days before the wedding. Now she just had to become accustomed to a new home and the most luxurious house she had ever lived in. In ten minutes she returned and Marek looked up. "I win," he said.

To her surprise, Noah still sat quietly in Marek's arms. "You do have a magic touch. Although his eyelids are getting droopy."

"Doesn't matter. I win."

"Then you'll just have to come collect your prize later when he's tucked in bed."

"You can count on it," Marek replied and returned to reading in a softer voice. Noah blinked and closed his eyes.

"That hardly counts because you just barely won," she said. "He's fallen asleep."

"There's no such thing as barely winning. A win is a win whether barely or by a mile. I definitely won and soon I expect to claim my prize."

"I still don't know how you held his attention for that long," she said, looking at her sleeping child.

"You come sit on my lap and I'll get your attention for just as long. I can do things that will make you sleep like a baby. Later."

She smiled. "Although that's a tempting offer, for now, I'll pass."

"You're missing out on a great deal of—" he paused a moment "—of something you won't forget and you'll enjoy immensely. I promise."

She fanned herself with her hand. "I do believe I've married a very sexy man," she said in a sultry voice. "Your self-assurance is about to overwhelm me," she added in a normal tone. "I'll take Noah to bed."

"It's just like you said you wanted." Marek stood easily. "I'll take him. You can come with us."

The sleeping baby snuggled against Marek's shoulder as he carried him to the nursery, which was near the master bedroom suite and adjoined the bedroom suite where Camille stayed. Marek glanced at her. "See, we can be a family for him. This is good, Camille. This is very good for him."

"I know it is, and that's why I agreed," she answered solemnly.

"Don't sound so unhappy about it."

"I've had him all to myself. There are moments this whole change seems overwhelming. The fear passes swiftly, and then I feel better about what we're doing."

"I'm glad. Also, guess what—he can say da-da."

She stopped to stare at Noah. "No kidding. You've taught him to say da-da," she said, laughing softly.

"Might have."

Marek put Noah into his crib gently, turning to place his arm around Camille as she stood close beside him. They both looked at the sleeping baby. "I suppose every mother thinks her baby is the most beautiful baby in the whole world. I love him with all my heart," she said.

"That's the thing about love—there's always room for more. I already love him, but he constantly reminds me of Kern and I know that's part of the reason. A delightful part," Marek added.

"I'm glad." She smoothed wispy hair on Noah's head, then turned and left the room. Her pulse was more erratic as they returned to the family area.

Marek faced her, encircling her waist with his arm. "I collect my winnings. I've been waiting and looking forward to claiming my prize."

Her heart skipped a beat as she gazed up at him. His attention was on her mouth, and he leaned closer. She inhaled, her heart pounding, and then his mouth covered hers, opened hers, and she lost awareness of everything else.

Wrapping her arms around his neck, she returned his kiss. As his kiss became more passionate, his arms tightened around her.

In a light, sizzling caress, his hand roamed over her bottom and along her leg, sliding beneath her shorts to caress her bare thigh. In seconds his hand slipped beneath her T-shirt, warm on her skin, his callused palm slightly rough as he unfastened the front snap of her bra and then cupped her breast.

Wanting to touch him, she moaned softly in pleasure. She was overwhelmed by caresses, hot kisses, touches, his fingers delving, intimacy enveloping them. Whether he realized it or not, each contact brought them closer. Loving caused sensations to bombard her, and she wanted to stir the same responses in him. Sliding her hands beneath his shirt, she felt the slight mat of chest hair that tickled her palm. Trailing both hands lightly over him, she tugged his shirt. He paused to raise his head and yank it off.

Watching her intently with desire blazing in the depths of his eyes, he pulled away her T-shirt and tossed it aside. He cupped her breasts, circling each lightly as she gasped and closed her eyes.

The slightest touch heightened desire, but the closeness, opening herself to him, carried with it a bonding that she couldn't continue to fight. Love had blossomed, and every physical stroke increased desire but also locked her heart more securely in his possession. There was no turning back from this now. They were legally wed, husband and wife.

His closeness with Noah tonight had captured her heart more than ever before.

She moaned softly, partly in pleasure, partly in frustration for a love that was totally one-sided.

As he unfastened her shorts she closed her fingers around his wrists and made an effort to stop kissing him. "Marek, wait a minute."

He watched her through hooded eyes and slowly raised his head, breathing deeply as if he had run a marathon.

"I know we're married and we can go to bed as husband and wife, but that's meaningless in matters of the heart. I have to go slowly into this or I'll hurt badly."

"Whenever you say no, I'll honor it, Camille. I promised I never wanted to hurt you. I mean that, and I intend to hold to it as much as humanly possible."

She closed her eyes, rocking on her heels, thinking his words just made her fall a bit more in love with him while nothing she did could even cause a tiny crack in the wall of ice that enveloped his heart.

He held her lightly and showered her with feathery kisses. "Don't worry. We're doing better together than I had expected. Our marriage is working far more than I dreamed possible. You're becoming a friend, helping me with the rough moments."

"Thank you and I'm glad," she said, thinking his statements heightened how much she liked him. "I know you've had some really bad moments because none of this, this bargain marriage, the relationship—you never expected or dreamed you would have anything like this in your life."

"Damn straight, there," he said, letting out a long breath. She was pulling herself together, and she stepped out of his arms to grab up her bra and T-shirt, pulling them on swiftly with her back turned to him.

Turning around she found him watching her intently. He

had made no effort to pull on his T-shirt, and she couldn't keep from surveying his chest, which made her breath catch and started her pulse pounding again. When she glanced up, his gaze had narrowed slightly.

"Knowing you and having this paper marriage has been good and that's partly because of you. Noah is the other factor in making this workable. He's an adorable baby."

"I have to agree with that. He likes you."

"He should. I love him already," Marek said softly.

"Don't make me fall in love with you," she whispered, knowing it was far too late for that request.

He stepped close again to slip his arms lightly around her waist. "I don't think you will. You're vulnerable and so am I, because neither of us have had a physical relationship in a long time. When you get back to being onstage, you'll forget me a good part of the time. I don't think there's any danger of either one of us falling in love. That will never be part of the equation, and we both can be open about it, which is also refreshing."

His words stung, and she hoped he never realized her growing feelings because he obviously did not return such emotions and didn't think he ever would. Unfortunately, her heart responded whether there was reciprocation or not.

Trying to lighten the situation, she smiled. "I think we were headed somewhere when we started this."

"We'll sit and talk if you want." He draped his arm casually across her shoulders and walked to the sofa to sit close, turning to face her. "I want all of you to live on the ranch when your schedule allows it. You might as well get accustomed to the ranch. I love it. I'm a rancher, a cowboy. Living that far from town will be different for you."

"It'll be a monumental difference since we've always lived in a city," Camille replied. "It's going to be a huge change for my sister."

"She'll be paid well," he remarked drily. "Sometimes that helps ease the change. Does Ashley want to go back for this fall semester?"

"Because of all the changes in our lives, she's agreed to wait until the January semester starts. Remember, tomorrow one of your jets is flying her home to Saint Louis for the rest of this week."

His gaze traveled over her features slowly. She reacted to the sensual study that held almost as much impact as physical contact. She forgot their conversation and was lost in his dark eyes.

He leaned closer and she could no more resist than if she had been hypnotized as she bent toward him. When his lips brushed hers, she closed her eyes, circling his neck with her arm. She paused only briefly. "We weren't going to do this."

"We haven't for a while," he whispered back.

He lifted her to his lap to embrace her. His arousal was hard against her hip, a throbbing reminder of his heated desire.

"Marek," she whispered, and his mouth on hers stopped her from talking. After a few minutes she pushed against him and gazed at him.

He pulled his head back slightly to look into her eyes. "You'll be mine soon, Camille," he whispered, and her heart thudded.

"Be careful, Marek. I'm going to melt that ice that encompasses your heart. You possess my heart, but you're making yours vulnerable to the fires we generate," she warned. "I want you to want me with all your being," she whispered, barely aware of what she said, uncertain that he even heard her, much less gave any thought to what she was telling him.

He kissed her hard, his tongue playing over hers and going deep, possessively, as he pulled her tightly against him.

Winding her fingers in his hair, she kissed him in return.

Finally, she slipped off his lap and walked away. "I should call it a night."

"Not at all. Sit and talk. It's early. We don't have a full day tomorrow. I'll send Ashley in the limo to the plane. Ginny and the girls will come to get Noah. We'll do what we want."

"You're right," she said, sitting slightly farther from him on the sofa.

"How did you decide on the name Noah?" he asked, his dark eyes holding passion.

"That was my grandfather's name. He's named for my grandfather and for his own father," Camille answered while trying to calm and wishing her voice wasn't as breathless.

"Does your dad mind being skipped over?"

"No, one of the granddaughters is named for him. Chelsea Taylor Avanole."

"Nice name. I'm glad you gave Noah Kern's name. I remember your text from Kern. The name made Kern happy. When he's old enough, I'll get a small, gentle horse for Noah. Long before that he can ride with me."

"I can't imagine my baby on a horse," she said. "You and I know little about each other's worlds."

"That makes life interesting," Marek said, smiling at her and moving closer. "And you're too far away," he said, slipping his hand lightly on her nape. "I'll take you to a rodeo and we'll also go dancing sometime and you can learn the two-step if you don't already know it. When you see the ranch house, just remember that we can remodel and redecorate any way you want. This is my house that I had built, and it's not old and filled with sentimental memories."

She listened and watched him while he talked, only half hearing what he told her, remembering their kisses and fighting the urge to reach out and touch him. If she did, she would be in his arms again.

In her wildest imaginings, she had never expected to have

a marriage of convenience, a honeymoon without making love, a husband who didn't love her. Yet they were getting to know each other and there was a physical attraction that neither one of them could resist.

It was two o'clock when she stood. "Now I do have to go to bed. I'm sleepy," she said, picking up an empty glass to take to the kitchen.

He went with her, and as they walked to her new bedroom that adjoined his with closed double doors between them, he draped his arm across her shoulders to draw her against him.

"You're not staying in here tonight," she whispered.

"I know I'm not," he replied. He gazed down at her. "Guard your heart well, Camille. Mine is frozen, and, make no mistake, it won't thaw."

"I've got your warning," she whispered. "I'll take care of myself."

He kissed her lightly and left.

Marek walked to his room, his thoughts on Camille. He would never fall in love and already she had a starry-eyed look and was telling him this would mean more to her with each kiss. He should leave her alone, but that was impossible. She was a desirable, beautiful woman, now his wife, as legally binding as any marriage.

Startled, he realized he was coming back to life fully. It still surprised him how much and how fast she had brought him out of his grief. How huge the transformation since the day Camille had walked into his office! The diminishing of his heartache had been subtle, gradual, but he was less steeped in heartbreak, each week more lusty. Camille was filled with life, her passion for living spilling over onto all around her, including him. He rubbed the back of his neck and wondered where they would be in this relationship a year from now.

Images and memories of Camille returned full force: of Camille in his arms, of kissing her, of her soft lips, of her body, dancing the samba with her and her seductive moves. The memories set his pulse racing and sent his temperature soaring. Maybe someday he would fall in love with her—something that seemed impossible now, but she had brought about changes he would have thought impossible three months ago.

It shocked him how much he wanted her. A month ago, he was completely oblivious to women. But from the moment Camille had slipped into his life, hot, passionate, she had stirred responses from him he hadn't known he could possibly give again. On their honeymoon he'd wanted her. If she had cooperated they would have consummated their marriage. Even now, he was certain it was only a matter of time before he seduced her. She was a passionate, hot-blooded woman and they were just getting to know each other. He thought her reluctance would melt away because she was responsive to his slightest touch, flirting with him, physically aware of him.

Noah had contributed, too, in bringing him back into the world fully. The baby was adorable, and Marek would do anything to get a laugh out of his tiny nephew, soon-to-be-adopted son. Already he loved the baby as much as if he were his own. If only Kern could have known Noah—how much Kern would have loved the little fellow.

Marek prayed Camille accepted all of their arrangements and let him have a lot of time with Noah. "Kern, you have a fine son," he said to no one. "I'll do my best for him."

Marek showered, climbed into bed and lay in the dark still thinking about the monumental changes in his life, thinking about holding Camille and making love to her.

He slept only a few hours and rose to dress, pulling on fresh jeans and a navy knit shirt. When he entered the kitchen he gave a swift appraisal of Camille in jeans and a red T-shirt. Her hair was caught behind her head in a red ribbon. She smiled and returned to feeding Noah and talking to Ashley, who was already back from visiting her friend. Her bags for her trip to Saint Louis were packed, ready by the door.

Half an hour after Ashley left for the airport, Ginny and her girls arrived to pick up Noah. She got instructions from Camille while Marek loaded the car with Noah's things. The girls hovered over Noah, who seemed happy with their attention.

As they drove away, Marek stood on the porch with his arm around Camille's shoulders. As Ginny and the girls waved, Marek and Camille waved in return.

"Thanks for letting them take him." Marek looked down at her. "Don't worry about him. He'll have everyone's undivided attention, and Ginny is an experienced mom. The girls have found a real live doll to play with. The whole family will hover over him like he's suddenly been crowned king of the world. They're only a thirty-minute drive away here in Dallas if you just can't stand being parted from him."

Camille smiled nervously as they walked back into the house together. "I won't worry. I felt ridiculous giving your sister instructions. She's had two girls and knows more about parenting than I do."

"You're used to Noah. All little kids are different."

"Says the man who told me he knew nothing about babies."

"You remember that? That was the first week we met."

"I remember everything about you."

"Do you really?" Marek turned her to face him. "Have you noticed?"

"Noticed what?" she asked, wondering what she had missed. "You have a new haircut?"

"No. We're home alone. A moment I've been looking forward to for some time. Guess why?" His heartbeat raced in anticipation that had built all morning. He looked into her compelling blue eyes.

"I believe the look in your eyes gives away your answer, but I'll ask. Why?"

"So I can do this," he said, drawing her into his embrace.

She tilted her head to give him access to her mouth. He leaned closer, brushing her lips with his, a teasing stroke that caused her lips to part.

"I want you, Camille," he whispered before his mouth came down on hers.

Eight

His tongue toyed with hers, fanning fires deep within her, making her want more of him. Her faint moan was barely audible in her own ears because of her roaring pulse.

They were alone, husband and wife. He had said he could never love again, and she was fully aware this was lust and went no deeper emotionally for him, but they were married. How much had he changed since their first night out? How much would he continue to change?

She framed his face with her hands and opened her eyes to look at him. His breathing was heavy and his eyes half-lidded with a sensual look that conveyed his intentions more than ever. His brow furrowed slightly. "What?"

"You've been up front with your warnings, Marek," she whispered. "I'll give you one. Guard your heart. If we continue, you may fall in love."

A harsh, shuttered look changed his expression. "There's no chance of that—"

She covered his mouth with hers, pressing her lips slowly on his, catching his lower lip lightly in her teeth to stroke slowly with her tongue. He inhaled, gave a conflicted moan as he tightened his arm around her and pulled her hard against him.

His thick erection reinforced his scorching gaze. She slid against him, lowering herself from tiptoe to flat-footed, sliding slowly, sensually along his hard body. Desire pounded in her, a heated longing for total commitment from him. "Marek, I've been to a doctor. I'm on the pill."

He kissed away further conversation. Yanking off his shirt, he tossed it away. While he kissed her, her fingers drifted lightly over him, tracing his sculpted chest muscles, bulging biceps, his hipbones. In feathery caresses her fingers trailed along his upper thighs in her fascination with his body, in her need to be as intimate as possible.

His raspy breathing deepened while his tongue was erotic, heightening her need.

Twisting her hips slowly, inching them over him so he would become aware of all of her, she let one hand drift toward the inside of his thigh and then trail higher.

He leaned away. His midnight eyes flamed with desire, a promise in just a look. Her heartbeat raced while he slipped his fingers beneath her shirt, moving with a tantalizing slowness that made her want to grasp his hands and place them on her tingling breasts as he watched her.

"Marek," she whispered, wanting to relay her feelings for him, to declare the love that built each day, but she held back, biting back words while she let her care flow into her kisses.

His fingers teased, heightening her desire as his hands caressed her full breasts, circling each and avoiding her taut peaks. Craving his touch, she leaned away to remove her shirt.

Inhaling deeply, he held her to look at her, slowly letting

his gaze consume each inch, making her quiver and ache with desire. With deliberation he pulled away the ribbon holding her hair, caressing her nape as he released the ribbon.

"You're beautiful."

"Marek," she said, tugging his shoulders to bring him closer, but he still held her away. He leaned down, his tongue trailing lightly on her throat, down between her breasts, circling underneath as his fingers had. Warm, wet, his tongue heightened her quivering need. Her nipples throbbed, and she grasped his wrists to hold his hands, looking down at him.

With lips swollen from passion and his eyes black from desire, his gaze consumed her while his hands persisted in fiery torment. Desire overwhelmed her, burning, pouring over every inch.

"Touch me," she whispered.

"I want you to really want my hands, my mouth on you," he whispered, showering kisses on her throat and lower.

She framed his head in her hands, tangling her fingers in his thick hair to draw him closer, to place his mouth, his kisses, where she wanted.

"Marek," she cried out in pleasure, gasping and throwing her head back as she clung to him and was immersed in sensation. Desire centered low in her. She thrust her hips against him and caressed him, her fingers shaking as she tried to yank his belt free and shove away the last clothing between them.

He stepped back to do the task himself, still watching her with hooded eyes, a blatant look that made her want to draw him close against her.

With deliberation she unfastened her slacks and let them fall, stepping out of them to kick away her sandals. His chest expanded as he drew a long breath, his gaze roaming slowly over her.

She hooked her fingers in the bikini panties, drawing them

slowly down, spreading her legs slightly as she stepped out of the bit of lace.

With a groan that conveyed both need and urgency, he drew her to him. His fingers were everywhere, following the course of his scrutiny and then moving where his gaze could not go between her thighs.

His mouth covered hers again, his tongue sliding over hers with tantalizing deliberation while his fingers toyed with her intimately. Writhing with pleasure, she clung to his broad shoulders, a sensuous thrust of her hips against his hand as she opened her legs farther to give him more access.

While he kissed her, his hands worked magic, making her want him more than she ever had, more than she would have dreamed possible.

"Marek, wait," she whispered, breaking away with an effort, giving him an intense look before she went down to take his thick rod to caress and kiss him. As his fingers combed through her long hair again, he shuddered, closing his eyes to let her love him with slow deliberation.

She wanted him to burn with need, to be totally aware of her and want her with every fiber of his being. If she could never have his love, she could have his body.

He leaned down slightly to put his hands beneath her arms and pull her up to gaze into her eyes. "Someday I'll have your heart," she whispered.

"You've been warned," he whispered in return before he kissed away any reply she might have wanted to make.

So have you, she mused as he kissed away rational thought. She held him tightly while he pulled her bottom up even more against him as they kissed. Passionate kisses increased desire until she wanted to hold him tightly, wrap her arms around him and urge him to fill her, to make love with her.

He swept her into his arms, walked to the bedroom and

placed her on the bed. As he eased beside her, he continued caressing and kissing her. She wanted him with all her being. Their lovemaking had driven her swiftly over the edge. Running her hands over him, she caressed him, trying to drive him to as great a need as she felt.

So many things had been life altering between them— just meeting and informing him about Noah, then marrying him—something in her wildest dreams she had never expected. Now their lovemaking was taking them to a new level—a change from which there would be no going back.

He moved over her, trailing his tongue and kisses down, circling each nipple and then taking each taut peak into his mouth to taste and kiss.

When he shifted lower, his hand slipped over her thighs. While he showered kisses over her belly, she writhed in pleasure beneath him. His tongue toyed with her lush breasts, his fingers creating intimate pleasure, teasing, heightening her need until her pulse pounded and she clung to him, crying out for him in urgency.

"Marek, come here."

"I'm here, and you're fantastic," he said, moving between her legs to trail more kisses along the inside of her thighs.

She cried out eagerly, her fingers winding in his hair while her hips arched to meet him as if seeking more of him.

"I want you," she gasped, knowing he could never guess the extent of what she felt.

He placed her legs over his shoulders, leaning down to tease the honeyed place, stirring up a wilder storm of passion. Pausing to watch her intently, he kissed the inside of her thigh. "I'm loving you until you're screaming for me," he whispered before he dipped between her legs and his tongue ended any rational thought.

"Love me now! I don't want to wait."

"I want you to want me more than you ever thought possible," he said.

"I want you with all my being," she whispered, arching her back, absorbed by desire. She gasped for breath. "Marek."

Her eyes flew open and she met his gaze, saw his intent and closed her eyes, wanting him and unable to wait longer. He eased partially into her, slowly filling her, a hot, hard torment more erotic than all else. Then he slipped away in a sensuous move that increased her need. She arched to meet him, and he entered her again.

She arched beneath him, crying out in longing and pleasure as they rocked together until urgency overwhelmed her.

Certain he held back to pleasure her, she thrust her hips faster until she felt his control shatter. His hips rocked with hers, tension reaching the ultimate peak. She cried out as rapture enveloped her and she soared with pleasure.

He followed, thrusting in a wild release that wracked him with spasms. His weight came down heavy, masculine, welcome. She held him tightly, feeling their hearts pound together.

"You're mine, my husband," she whispered, certain he wouldn't hear her.

"Ah, Camille, my love, this is good. I never thought this possible. You've taken me to paradise."

Flowery words, precious, intimate moments. She meant everything she said and she could only wish that he did, too. She ran her fingers through his hair, watching black locks spring away. "You're a handsome man, Marek Rangel. And an incredibly sexy one."

He smiled, showering light kisses on her face and throat. "You win that prize. I want to keep you in my arms all night long."

"If you do, you know what will follow."

"I have no idea. Let's try it and see what happens," he said, teasing her.

She smiled at him while she ran her fingers over his jaw, feeling the stubble that was beginning to show. "You're a handsome devil, Marek Rangel."

"And you're stunning," he said. He rolled to his side, taking her with him, and they faced each other while he smiled with satisfaction.

"This is a good marriage, Camille. We'll be good for Noah."

She laughed. "You say that only days since our wedding. It hasn't been a month yet. You can't tell whether this is good or bad."

"Of course I can. You don't think it's good?"

"It's wonderful," she replied. "Noah is happy, and now he has a daddy, which I think is a fine thing for him. He'll have grandparents because Jess will be another grandfather, I suspect. He has aunts who love him, now more cousins."

"Ginny and her family are already crazy about him. In his quiet way, Jess is, too."

"I'm glad. I've told you in June I will perform *La Traviata* here in Dallas. I will sing Violetta's part. I want you to come for opening night."

"I'd be delighted," he said.

"If you don't care for opera after you've been to a performance, tell me. I know not everyone does. I won't burden you with attending again if you don't like it."

"I'm going to love watching you," he said and she smiled, shaking her head.

"You have no idea whether you will or not. Save the flowery declarations until you can say them truthfully."

He grinned. "I think I will love it. Afterward, will you come home?"

"Of course. There may be a party, but eventually I'll come home. You'll be with me, whatever I do."

"Then I'll be happy. I told you earlier, I've waited eons to be alone with you. It seemed this time would never arrive."

"You wasted no time when they all left," she remarked drily.

"If you knew how much I've thought about making love to you, you'd know why I wasted no time." He propped his head on his hand. "Want to shower or sit in a hot tub and relax?"

"When you put it that way, the hot tub wins."

Standing, he picked her up and she wound her arm around his neck. "You're a feather."

She laughed. "Hardly. It takes a body to have the voice I have. No feather here."

"A gorgeous, lush, to-die-for beauty," he said, carrying her to his sunken tub. She watched as he began to fill the tub and shortly they both sat with her in front of him, between his legs, while he caressed her lightly, toyed with long strands of her hair and talked about growing up spending a lot of his life on his grandfather's ranch.

He carried her back to bed and made love to her again, loving her through the night. Afterward she stayed in his embrace, still talking about their lives before they had met each other. He asked about her career, and she could feel a closer bonding with him. Did he feel the same or was this a casual conversation that he would forget swiftly?

He rolled on his side, holding her close with one arm while he propped his head on his other hand. "Camille, we're married. Share a bedroom with me."

Startled, she gazed into his inscrutable dark eyes. "I'm surprised you want that," she said, giving herself time to think, but also admitting the first thought that came to mind. This was not something she had expected, and her heart leaped. Could this mean that he cared more for her?

"I've given it thought. Our sex life is fantastic," he declared in a husky voice, brushing a kiss on her lips. "I like having you in my arms and in my bed. I would like that on a regular basis. We're husband and wife—why not? We are making love and it's good. I like being with you. It's that simple."

A mixture of feelings gripped her. His declaration and invitation to sharing a bedroom meant a big shift in their relationship. She loved him, and her deepest reaction was joy. Along with it was awareness of all she had worked to achieve. What would a closer relationship, her growing love for him, do to her career?

Was her relationship with Marek a threat to her career? She might be reading more into his actions than she should, but this was a wonderful change in so many ways. The more she could be intimate with him, the more they were simply together and enjoyed each other's company, the more likely he was to lose that barrier around his heart. There was a far better chance of his falling in love if they lived together as husband and wife.

But if he did, could she cope with Marek's demands and the demands of her career?

She had to follow her heart.

She shifted slightly to wrap her arm around him. "Yes, I will move in with you."

Pleasure flared in his expression, and he kissed her long and deeply. In seconds, caressing began and the conversation was temporarily over.

When they were finally back in bed, in each other's arms, Marek faced her and brushed long strands of hair away from her face. "When do you want to move to my bedroom? Tonight?"

She laughed. "I think I am 'in.' Perhaps it will be easier when I move to the ranch."

"Fine with me," he said, looking contented. "I like this. It'll be better. You'll see."

"I don't believe you heard any argument from me," she said, amused by his remarks.

He looked startled and then smiled faintly. "That's good. We're in agreement. Noah will like it, too."

She laughed. "Noah wouldn't care if we camped out at separate ends of your ranch."

Marek had to grin. "Maybe not, but he will have fun being with both of us at the same time."

"I'll agree with you there, too."

"This is good, Camille. Very good."

"Don't sound so surprised," she said, finger combing his dark hair away from his face.

"I am surprised. I never expected to find happiness in this marriage, much less to have it happen so swiftly."

Her heart skipped a beat again, and more pleasure filled her. "I'm glad. Some of it has surprised me. We took some risks."

He gave her a piercing look and then his expression changed as his gaze shifted to her mouth. He leaned down to kiss her and pull her closer.

It was dawn when she lay in his arms with her head against his shoulder and their bodies pressed close. She looked at him and saw the steady rise and fall of his chest. For the first time in her life she was in love. She was more deeply in love with him each day. In so many ways, he captured her love, her heart, her respect, giving her joy and excitement. She expected him to be a wonderful dad for Noah.

Where was she headed with him? She hadn't been able to prevent falling in love. How much could she steal his affections and bind his heart to hers? If she did, could she cope with the love of a man shared with pursuit of a career?

Through the days while they were alone at the house, they made love often with neither of them leaving the house for anything. When Ginny called, Camille longed to have Noah home again. Since Ginny and the girls sounded so overjoyed to have him, she would not do anything to cut his visit short. Once when they finished the call, Marek turned to her.

"You've given them the most blessed gift. They love Noah, and you can hear how happy they are to have him visit. I know it's hard for you because you're not accustomed to being separated. Thank you," he said with so much sincerity, she was touched.

"I'm glad they love him. It's good for him to get to know his new family. I want him loved by all his family."

His gaze lowered to her mouth and he leaned closer. His kiss ended their conversation.

Late the next morning, Marek stepped out of bed. "Don't go away. We need to talk business and I'll be right back."

Mystified, she sat up and pulled a sheet beneath her arms.

Shortly he returned with papers under his arm and a tray with glasses of orange juice and cups of coffee.

She laughed. "Marek, it's almost noon and you're bringing breakfast in bed."

"Not a complete breakfast, but a partial one." He handed her the tray. "Hold everything while I get back beside you." He sat and took a cup of coffee and a glass of orange juice to place on a bedside table. "You can put yours next to your side of the bed."

"Thank you," she said, sipping the orange juice after she had placed the steaming coffee on the table. "What on earth do we have to do?"

"We have to childproof my ranch house fast."

She laughed. "He isn't walking yet."

"I want to be ready when he does. I want you to look at some designs and you can help pick one out. We need gates on some of the doors and where there are steps. I want a play area for Noah with a slide and swings."

She laughed. "Marek, wait until he walks. He can get something like that for Christmas."

"I might want to swing him. Babies like to swing."

"In little baby swings. Let's look at the brochures."

For the next hour they pored over plans and brochures and talked about decorators and builders. Finally Marek took all the pamphlets and notes and dropped them over the side of the bed to the floor.

"Good. We'll pick something out and I can have it installed so it'll be in place when we get there. "I want to get the ranch house so it's safe and comfortable for you and Noah because I want you to love it the way I do."

She looked at him and he turned to study her. "What?" he asked.

"You're turning into a great daddy. I'm amazed."

"What did you think I was, some kind of ogre?"

"Of course not, but you knew nothing about kids and he's not your baby actually—"

Placing one finger on her lips, Marek silenced her.

"He's my baby now, Camille. I love him already. I want to start the adoption procedure as soon as we possibly can, and my attorney has been getting it lined up. I'll be Noah's dad and I want his last name legally changed to Rangel." He put his arm around her shoulders. "We'll be a real family."

"That's fine with me," she answered. "That's what I expected from what you have already said."

They gazed into each other's eyes, and her heart began to beat faster as the air thickened and desire blazed again.

He placed his hand lightly on one side of her face. "This is so damn good. I never dreamed it would be like this," he whispered, before his mouth crushed hers and she forgot about fences and swings.

Monday they flew to the ranch on one of Marek's jets. As she looked below, Camille marveled at the changes in her life. She was more in love than ever with Marek, a love that grew daily, and he didn't have a clue. He sat beside her, dressed in a Western long-sleeve cotton shirt, tight jeans, a hand-tooled leather belt and Western boots, looking every inch the handsome, rugged cowboy. It was as foreign to her way of life as someone from another planet. Even so, right now, she longed to reach out and touch him, to hold his hand or even just flirt with him, but they weren't alone.

She had chased stardom all her life. Now she pursued a man's love. Marek had so much to give—and she wanted to give to him. His hurts would heal if he would open his heart and let in love.

She looked at her sleeping baby in his carrier, which was buckled securely. Noah wore a pale blue jumper and white shirt and she thought he looked adorable and angelic. Noah was blissfully unaware of where he was going or how his life had changed. He definitely had taken to Marek, and it was mutual. She had been astounded to discover how much Marek cared for Noah.

Wrapped in her own world, Ashley sat reading college brochures. Camille was happy for her whole family as they changed their lives and began to do what they wanted. Her mother would retire from teaching after the coming year and then she could spend more time with Noah. Now her brother could afford college easily. When they had last talked, Stephanie had bought a condo in Saint Louis and was acquiring new furniture.

Camille glanced out the window, looking at the sprawling land below. Her future was difficult to imagine in so many ways. Her attention returned to Marek. He was changing, but to what extent? He turned to look at her and arched one dark eyebrow.

"What?" he asked.

"Just wondering what you're thinking?"

"Thinking about you mostly, but I've been going over ranch finances," he said, putting away the papers in his lap. "Looks as if Ashley's getting prepared to enroll. I'm not going to have to change my schedule on looking for a new nanny, am I?"

"No, we won't. You won't be getting one on your own, either. She's trying to work out a way to take classes online and then go for those short, intense classes so she can continue as nanny until Noah gets older."

He glanced at Ashley, who was concentrating on her reading. "I'm sure you'd feel better if she stayed on longer."

"I would. I'm trying to stay out of it and let her make her own decision without any pressure from me. She came up with this plan on her own. Of course, I'm delighted because he's so little. When he's gets bigger and can talk, I'll feel better about hiring a nanny and letting her go. My parents wish they could spend more time with Noah, but they both work full-time."

"That will change for your mom. You'll be able to afford to help them."

"We have so many changes in our lives."

"I hope you like the ranch and life there. To me, it's the best place on earth."

"I won't know until I try," she said, but it was difficult to imagine the life awaiting her.

"I told Zeb to fly over the ranch so you can see it from the air."

"I'll tell Ashley. That will be fun to see," she said, turning to her sister.

When Marek finally told her they were flying over the ranch, she and Ashley both turned to the windows. Marek leaned close, his shoulder touching hers. "I think you can tell the main house where I live."

"There's a town below."

"No, that's the ranch."

"Ashley, Marek said the ranch is below," Camille said, unable to take her eyes off the structures spread below. "You have a palace. It's huge, and there's an enormous swimming pool. Why all the homes near your house?"

"For staff. Jess has one."

"This isn't what I imagined at all," Camille said, astounded at everything she saw below. "You have your own small town."

"Not quite," he said, laughing. "It's home and I love it. I'm going to love having you in it."

She smiled at him, happy about his statement.

The plane headed south and she sat back, astonished by what she had seen.

"All of that belongs to you?" Ashley asked, looking dismayed.

"Yes, it does. You'll like it, Ashley. You'll see."

They landed in town and then climbed into a waiting limo for the drive to the ranch, which took almost as long as the flight had taken.

They sped along a deserted gray ribbon of highway, passing land covered with feathery mesquite bent from the prevailing south winds. Green cacti sprouted across the land beneath the mesquite.

The moment the ranch house loomed in sight, Camille's breath stopped and she gazed out the window. Stunned, she looked at a one-story palatial home that looked far bigger from the ground than it had from the air. "My heavens," she gasped softly, turning to look again at the powerful rancher she had married.

Nine

The ranch house and other structures spread in all directions with wings built on the mansion. The ranch revealed Marek's power and wealth far more than the Dallas home, which had been lavish, comfortable and well-appointed. This was a town with an enormous home at the center.

When she glanced at Marek, he looked back at her with his eyebrows arching. "What?" he asked.

"More than ever, your ranch is an indication of your immense wealth," she said. She didn't add power, but she shuddered slightly, reminded again how easily he could take her to court now to get custody of Noah. By marrying Marek, she had given him far more control over her baby.

Smiling at her, he reached over to take her hand. "Stop looking at me as if I'd just grown fangs. I'm the same person and, basically, a cowboy. All the buildings serve ranch purposes or are homes for my staff and the cowboys who work for me."

"It's an enormous compound."

"It seems large because you're unaccustomed to it. The first thing I'd like to show you is our bedroom," he said, desire plain in the depths of his dark eyes.

"That may have to wait until later," she answered, a breathlessness coming into her voice along with eager anticipation. His innuendo was plain. He was beginning to flirt more, making more innuendos. Subtle changes in him were surfacing and she wondered about their significance. Were his feelings shifting, too?

He held her hand and she glanced down, looking at their entwined fingers. More and more he casually hugged her, held her hand, touched her. He spent time with her when he was home. How important was she in his life? And there was also the persistent worry: if he ever fell in love, could she cope with a commitment that would complicate her career? It was a small problem next to how much she wanted his love. She was confident if there was mutual love, she could work through the complications.

They went through another tall iron gate, this one closed with a code to punch to open the gate. In minutes the limo rolled through and shortly they approached the main house, a sprawling stucco structure with north and south wings.

The yard had a tall, ornate iron fence surrounding well-kept grounds with tall shade trees and beds of colorful spring flowers. Red, pink and purple crepe myrtle bushes flanked the front porch that ran the length of the house. In front of the house was a pond with three fountains.

They circled the house, driving around and passing a corral with a large barn. Beyond it were rows of stables and another corral. Buildings and houses could be seen farther to the north. Beyond the well-kept yard the land returned to the wild mesquite and cacti she had seen on the drive from the airport.

When she had told Ashley she would move into his bedroom, her sister had arched her eyebrows. "Is that what you want?"

"Yes, it is," Camille answered.

"You're in love with him," Ashley said.

"How'd you know?" Camille asked her, surprised. "Does it show?"

"I know because I'm your sister. I don't think it's obvious otherwise. I don't think Stephanie ever noticed."

"Stephanie hasn't been around as much as you have."

"No, but I've known for a while. Since you came back from your honeymoon."

"I think before that," Camille admitted.

"I don't blame you. He's a great guy, Camille, and I hope he doesn't break your heart because he was so deeply in love with his late fiancée."

"I know. You can't control the feelings in your heart for someone."

"Try to take care of yourself."

"I have Noah to love—that keeps me from hurting too badly over anything else. I have my career. That will always take my thoughts off my private life," Camille answered, doubting if her career would be enough.

"I just pray you aren't hurt. He seems to have his heart completely locked away."

"I can't undo what I feel at this point."

"Well, as I said, just take care of yourself."

Camille gazed out the limo window. Would Marek cause her heartbreak?

When they parked to go inside, Ashley carried Noah. At the door, Marek picked up Camille. "Welcome home, Camille," he said in a husky voice. Her heart thudded. If only he meant what he said! She held him and gazed into dark eyes as he smiled at her and then carried her over the threshold

into an entryway. It was filled with hooks holding rain slick-
ers, two tall hat racks holding broad-brimmed Western hats,
boots lined neatly on the floor. He set her down.

"Come meet the staff, namely, my great cook and the man
who manages this place. I doubt if the others are around at
this hour."

Marek took Noah from Ashley, and they entered a large
kitchen that held stainless steel appliances and had an adjoining sitting room and an informal dining area with a brick
fireplace filling one corner.

A black-haired man in a white apron smiled at them. "Ladies, I want you to meet Hector Galban," Marek said. "Hector, meet my wife, Mrs. Rangel, her sister, Miss Avanole.
This is Noah," Marek said, turning the baby to show him
to the cook.

Camille smiled and said hello to a compact man who
looked more like he should be working with cattle on the
ranch than in the kitchen cooking for a living. Barrel-chested
with thick black curls, Hector greeted each one of them.
They chatted a moment and then entered a wide hallway
with a polished plank floor. Another man in black trousers
and white shirt appeared.

"This is Cletus Byrne, who is my house manager and
butler when I need one," Marek said, making introductions.

Camille greeted another man who looked as if he should
work out on the ranch instead of in Marek's house. He was
broad-shouldered and tall with sandy hair and a quiet manner.

"Cletus will get your things. We have a temporary nursery set up in a large bedroom where Ashley can stay with
Noah. Let's get settled and then I'll give you a tour of the
house," Marek said, carrying Noah as they walked toward
the front and down the wide hallway filled with oil paintings of Western art. In the wide entrance, a brass candelabra

caught the afternoon sunlight streaming through tall windows that flanked the front door.

"Marek, this is a beautiful home," Camille said. "Not exactly what I expected."

"I can imagine," he replied with amusement in his voice.

He took them to the temporary rooms for Ashley and Noah. "The master bedroom is at the end of the hallway, so you won't be far away. When we take the complete tour of the house, both of you can look at bedrooms and select where you want Noah's room. There will be a nursery with an adjoining playroom and a suite for Ashley."

They walked into a bedroom and sitting room filled with afternoon sunshine. Camille wandered through it, looking at the white furniture and the adjoining bathroom, which was enormous.

"This is beautiful," Camille said. "You've already got it ready for Noah. Maybe I should cancel the decorator."

"Not at all. I want a place fixed with Noah in mind. This already existed and it's not a nursery, not even a bedroom for a young boy. You've been planning and you and Ashley have talked about what you want with the decorator. We'll have him out here this week and get this moving."

"This is a wonderful place for Noah," Ashley said, circling the room that had been turned into a temporary playroom.

"Good. It'll have to do for the time being. I'll show you where we'll be," he said, taking Camille's arm.

Ashley turned. "You two go ahead. I'm going to change Noah and then I'll join you," she said.

Camille turned to go with Marek. When they were alone in his suite, she turned to him. "I think Ashley wanted to give us a moment to ourselves."

"That's fine with me," Marek replied. "I'd prefer the rest of the day and tonight," he said, placing his hands on her waist.

She smiled. "You'll have to wait."

"You can't imagine how reluctantly," he said, giving her another hot look that made her sizzle.

"If you wait, you'll appreciate me more," she added in a sultry voice, stepping away from him.

He inhaled deeply. "If I 'appreciate' you more, I'll go up in flames. You keep that up and I'm going to lose my self-control."

"Maybe I'm trying to keep 'that' up."

"Camille," he said in a husky voice, reaching for her again.

She smiled and walked away. "Ashley will join us soon. Now show me your bedroom."

He stared at her a moment in silence, desire burning in his gaze. "Our room," he said as if reminding himself. "You can also get the decorator and change our rooms however you like," he said. "All I ask on that is let me see the changes. I have an office of sorts in one corner and some things I still want to keep in there."

"Of course. I'm not changing anything in your room at this point. I won't without telling you, either."

When she stepped into the large sitting room, he pulled her to one side of the door. "Ashley hasn't come and you started this. We have a minute and we're married anyway," he said, embracing her and leaning down to kiss her. While her heartbeat jumped, she held him to kiss him in return.

"Welcome home, Mrs. Rangel," Marek whispered, framing her face with his hands. "Camille, you and Noah are the best possible things that could have happened. This marriage is great. Far more than I expected."

"I agree," she whispered, her heart racing over his declaration. How easy it would be to tell him she loved him, but she wouldn't, not until he made a declaration, if that ever happened. He was far from falling in love yet, but she had hope as long as they were happy together and he wanted to be with her and make love with her.

"Marek, Ashley really will join us in a minute," Camille said, stepping away from him but wanting to close the door and stay in the bedroom with him the rest of the night, which was impossible.

She looked around the rooms where she would now live. Like everything else, Marek's suite was appealing. The floors gleamed with polish and thick area rugs were centered in the sitting room and adjoining bedroom. The furniture was covered in navy leather with fruitwood and she saw his corner office held a rolltop desk that looked antique. One wall was filled with shelves of books, pictures, trophies, a collection of memorabilia. She crossed the room to pick up a picture of Marek and Kern. Both had Western hats pushed to the backs of their heads. Both were in boots, jeans and Western shirts. They casually had arms around each other's shoulders. A horse stood behind them, its head by Kern's shoulder.

"This is a good picture," she said.

Marek crossed the room and smiled. "Kern had just won that horse from me in a bet and he was delighted. It was worth losing to see him so ridiculously happy. He loved that roan and wanted it from the day I got it." Marek laughed and shook his head. "That was a fun time. One of the good memories."

He glanced at the shelf as she replaced the picture next to one of Jillian.

He picked up the picture to fold the back and lay it flat on the shelf. "I'll put away Jillian's pictures."

"You don't need to," Camille said, turning to him. "I truly don't mind. You loved her and you were going to marry her. I'll feel better because I imagine you like to see them."

"That's past and gone. I don't need the pictures to remember her and I can look at them if I want. I'll put them away. It'll probably help me to move on."

She didn't think he would have done any such thing before their wedding and honeymoon. He was changing, coming out of the shell, but how much would he open his heart in the future?

She walked around the room and roamed into the masculine bedroom, with a bed that had an old-fashioned high headboard and navy-and-white pillows and comforter.

"This room looks like you."

"You can change this however you want as long it isn't pink or purple. I can't do purple or pink."

She grinned. "Aw, shucks, imagine that," she said, teasing him, unable to imagine Marek sprawled in a pink bed.

They heard Ashley and went out to find her in the sitting room. She held out Noah and Camille took him.

"Give him to me and we'll have a quick tour," Marek said.

Marek showed them the gym, with an indoor pool of pale blue tiles with white Corinthian columns on each side. Next they went to the entertainment room. "Both of you—this is your home, too, now. Ashley, you and Camille both feel free to use these rooms, the gym, the entertainment center, the kitchen, the pool, anything you want whenever you want, middle of the night or whatever. This is your home now," he repeated, gazing at Camille.

"Thank you," Camille said.

"Come on, we'll continue this tour," he said. By the time they stepped outside on a patio that was as big as the central part of the house, Camille wondered if she would ever find her way around. She stopped and looked around at the outdoor living area stocked with what looked like indoor furniture with a well-equipped kitchen. Beyond the chairs and furniture and outdoor rooms was a fenced area with a cabana, a dazzling pool that had slides and fountains and beds of flowers and palm trees.

To one side of the yard was another waterfall, as well as a fish and lily pond that was equally gorgeous.

There was a play area with a portable fence already set up for Noah. It was large enough for adults so Ashley took Noah from Marek. Holding the baby she stepped into it with him and set him down, giving him his toys. She sat near him, playing with him.

Marek declared happy hour and served everyone the drink of her choice. When they all had drinks, Ashley lifted her daiquiri. She sat in the fenced area on a blanket with Noah beside her and toys spread in front of him. Rising to her feet, she said, "Here's to the best brother-in-law ever, besides being the only one I have," she added, smiling at Marek. "Thank you for coming into our lives. Noah will thank you a few years from now."

Marek stood and crossed to her, leaning over the plastic fence to touch his glass to hers. "I'll drink to that," he said, turning back to Camille to toast her glass as well. She sipped, looking over the rim of her glass at him and wanting to be alone with him. His dark eyes held her gaze, conveying a sensual promise for later that night.

Marek's cell phone rang, and he excused himself to answer it.

When he was out of earshot, Camille smiled at her sister. "That was a nice toast, Ashley."

"I meant it, Camille. He's been incredible."

"I think so," Camille answered.

"Don't let him break your heart," Ashley whispered, looking at Marek, whose back was turned.

"I just hope for the best, but he's being very good to us."

"Amen to that."

Marek returned with phone in hand. "Ginny's on the

phone. The girls want to have Noah back. Any chance of them keeping him again anytime soon? And feel free to say no."

"It's fine with me." Camille looked at Ashley, who glanced at Noah.

"If you two don't mind, I'll fly home to Saint Louis again this weekend. I could leave on Friday and get back Sunday night if that would be all right."

"My plane will take you. Actually, we can go to Dallas and spend the weekend there. Ashley will fly home and Ginny and the girls can take Noah. How's that?"

Camille laughed. "All of us flying to Dallas so two little girls—"

"And one big one," Marek interrupted.

"So they can play with Noah for a couple of days. I don't care. I'd like to spend the weekend in Dallas."

Marek raised his phone. "Ginny, we're not doing this every weekend, but we'll come back to Dallas. Ashley is going home to Saint Louis. We'll come early Friday and you can have him from Friday around noon until Sunday afternoon. How's that?" He held the phone away as squeals erupted.

Shaking his head, he said, "Tell the girls to calm down. They'll see a lot of him. Okay. See you Friday. I'll tell them."

He put away his cell phone and looked at Camille and Ashley. "Profuse thanks, ladies, for sharing Noah. I'm sure you could hear the girls' screams of joy that he's coming for the weekend." Marek glanced at Noah. "He's oblivious to all this hoopla. I may have to have a talk with my sister and tell her to get those girls new dolls or, better yet, get another baby in the family. Maybe you can pick out new dolls for them," he said to Camille.

Camille laughed. "The girls seemed totally fascinated with him and he likes them, but then, Noah likes everyone."

"He's Kern's son," Marek remarked. "Thanks again, hon," he said to Camille.

"He'll be happy," she replied, thinking of Marek's casual endearment. The *hon* was so lightly stated, yet the term was a warm, fuzzy blanket wrapping around her heart, making her feel that he cared about her.

Friday, Camille saw the Rangel jet take off with Ashley on board, headed to Saint Louis. In the next hour, she watched Ginny and the girls come by Marek's Dallas house to pick up Noah. Finally, Camille turned to look at Marek as he closed and locked the door behind his sister and her brood.

"We're alone," he said when he faced her. "Come here, Camille."

Monday when they returned to the ranch, Marek held Camille's hand on the plane. The weekend had been fabulous. The more he made love to her, the more he wanted her. That amazed him. In so many ways, from that first day he had met her, she had constantly surprised him.

June approached, when she would be locked into performing for two weeks, and he knew he would see almost nothing of her in that time. He didn't like the thought. When had she become important to him? It was as if he couldn't get through a day without her in his life.

He shifted to look at her. Camille was dressed in red slacks and a matching red silk blouse. A red scarf encircled her hair at the back of her neck. He wondered whether she was wearing red or black underwear, vowing to buy her something sexy soon. Very personal, very sexy. His blood heated at the thought. He glanced out the window without seeing anything. Was he falling in love with his wife? The question startled him. He had constantly credited his feelings for Camille to pure lust, but did it go beyond that? Had she replaced the void left in his heart? He would always love Jillian, but there was only a memory and a heartache over her loss. Camille was here, filled with zest and life.

Could he have already fallen in love with his wife without realizing it? He turned again to look at her. How he wished they were alone. He would like to take that red scarf off her hair and let the mass of midnight hair fall freely over her shoulders. He wanted to bury himself in her heat and softness. *Am I in love?* The question nagged at him as he stared at her. She turned to look at him. "You look deep in thought."

"I'm thinking about the changes we need to make at the ranch. We'll need a nursery that can easily be transformed into a suite for a little boy. You'll need a music room. We can do that."

"That I do want," she said, a somber note in her voice.

"Anything worrying you?"

She smiled. "Not at all. Just curiosity, and maybe I'm a little overwhelmed. My life is changing swiftly. You came into it like a bolt of lightning and absolutely fried my old life instantly."

He leaned closer to her. "I believe I can say the same thing. Mine is better now, Camille."

"That's the nicest possible thing you could say," she whispered.

"I mean it." He wished he could be alone with her because he wanted to say more, but this wasn't the time. He glanced away. Across the aisle, Ashley was buried in her brochures and books and Noah slept, unaware his life changed by the day now.

Marek ran his thumb lightly across Camille's knuckles, placing her hand on his thigh and putting his hand over hers as he sat back and gazed out the window. "We'll be there soon."

She had brought about the impossible in his life, something he thought he would never again experience. He wanted to scoop her up now and kiss her and it took all his control to sit and try to think clearly about when he could possibly first be alone with her.

That night Camille and Marek got Noah bathed and in his pajamas and Camille took him back to the family room to rock him to sleep.

Still marveling how much his life had changed, Marek sat watching them while the women talked softly. Camille's hair spread over one shoulder with the sleeping baby on the other. She was beautiful, and she had filled a void in his heart.

He studied her solemnly. Already, his relationship with her had gone where he never thought it would. He had never even considered the possibility that he would care for her to the extent his heart would be touched. She wasn't the woman to get involved with. Her heart was taken by her career. Would it be possible to get her to give up her career for a full, family-centered life? Already, he was deeply involved with her, and he wanted to be.

She stood and cradled the sleeping baby in her arms. Ashley jumped up. "I'll take him to bed. I'm turning in, anyway," she said, taking Noah as Marek stood. Camille brushed a kiss on the top of his head.

"'Night, Marek, 'night, Camille," Ashley said, leaving with Noah sleeping against her shoulder.

"So you've seen the ranch and spent a few days here now," Marek said, sitting close to Camille as she sat again on the sofa. "What would you like to remodel? Redecorate? Change?"

"I'm checking into the names of decorators you gave me about the nursery. I definitely want to change that whole suite so it looks as if it belongs to a little boy. I also need a music room. Other than that, I'm fine for now. I don't want to come in and change everything."

"The way you've changed me," he said, moving closer to her where he could wind his fingers in her hair. "I'm not the same person I was when I met you. I'm happy, Camille. So happy with you."

She leaned forward to brush his lips lightly with hers. His hand tangled in her hair, and he kissed her hard.

When she leaned away, she gasped for breath. "Maybe we should go back to discussing redecorating."

"Do what you want. End of discussion. This is much more interesting," he said, moving closer to slip his arm around her waist and kiss her.

She leaned forward to kiss him in return.

He released her. "Ashley's gone to bed. We can talk in our room. Let's go," he said, standing and holding out his hand. She took his hand to stroll through the house with him while he switched off indoor lights.

"I told you my schedule involved going to Saint Louis in September to see my family after I finish performing in August in Santa Fe. I'll amend that slightly. I'll come back here for two weeks and then go to Saint Louis for one."

"I can't argue with that," Marek replied.

When they stepped into his bedroom suite and he closed the door, he reached out to draw her against his chest. "I've wanted you in my arms all evening," he said in a husky voice, leaning closer to kiss her, thoughts of the future gone.

The following week they returned to Dallas and she threw herself into practice and lessons the majority of her waking hours to get ready for her upcoming performance of *La Traviata*.

Marek stayed in Dallas, dismayed by the amount of work she put into her practice. He heard her sing scales and exercises, but he left early to go to his office and returned in the evening to stay out of the way. He wouldn't have realized the full extent of her efforts except he phoned her during the day, avoiding the hours he knew she spent in rehearsal. Sometimes he would only to talk to her briefly, and then she would return to practice her voice lesson, or go over her lesson in getting her Italian correct for the performance. She also worked out each day and they began to work out at 6:00 a.m. together, just so he could see her during her waking hours. After seven in the evening was the only time she let go and played with Noah. Finally after everyone else had gone to bed, she would go with Marek to their bedroom. They made love for hours into the night the first two nights, but by the third, after making love, she fell into an exhausted sleep and he knew he should not wake her again, but let her have the rest she needed. By Thursday, he went back to the ranch to stay out of her way and not be a distraction because each day she poured herself more into her work.

As he twisted wire, working on mending a fence, he realized he was standing, staring into the distance, his thoughts totally focused on Camille. His heart thudded and he found it difficult to breathe. He was in love with Camille when he had been certain such a thing could never happen. He had lusted after her, admired her, seduced her, laughed with her, shared Noah with her, but he hadn't expected to fall in love with her.

From what she had told him, she was getting back to a normal routine, which meant she would not have as much time for him as she had been giving him through the wedding and right after. Had he gotten himself into a situation where he would only experience more hurt? He couldn't ask her to give up her career and be a rancher's wife. He couldn't give up the ranch and go back to city life and work in an office on a daily routine. They had agreed that sometimes he would travel with her, which would be good, but he couldn't do that all the time. He couldn't imagine spending his life following her from town to town. And he hated the separations. He missed her anytime that he was away from her now. How had she so ingrained herself in his heart?

Thinking about being with her, he had to admit it was love he felt. He didn't even know how long he had been in love with his wife. Maybe since their honeymoon. That's when she had broken through the barriers around his heart. He just hadn't realized how thoroughly she had. He hadn't recognized or stopped to think about his own feelings. Maybe it had even been before their honeymoon, a gradual thing that he hadn't recognized as it had been happening. A miracle for him.

He loved her. Totally, completely. And if he loved her, he wanted her in his life, not this piecemeal seeing each other between her voice lessons and, soon, her performances and trips home to her family. He wanted her in his life just as he had wanted Noah in his life. Each night he had missed her more than ever. Now, he sat thinking about how he could ask her to give up her career. He hated the absences, but he hated hurting her more. How could he ask her to give up what she'd worked so hard to achieve?

He had lost one love. Had he set himself up for another devastating heartbreak?

On the weekend he returned to Dallas. Ashley had flown home again, and Camille had agreed to let Ginny keep Noah Friday and Saturday nights and have him home with Marek Sunday night before Marek returned to the ranch.

Between Camille's full schedule in Dallas and their separation when he was at the ranch, he wondered about their future. As she succeeded in her career, she would probably be busier than she was now. Could he deal with that?

Monday, the last week of May, he stayed in Dallas and

told Camille he was going to his office. As soon as the stores opened, he called his jeweler and talked briefly before leaving for the jewelry store.

It was after six when Camille finished her daily routine and showered, dressing for dinner in black silk slacks and a matching sleeveless top.

Marek played with Noah in the room that had become a temporary nursery until the redecorating was finished. Seated cross-legged on the floor, Marek talked to Noah while playing patty-cake with him. Noah laughed and clapped his hands in imitation.

"Having fun?" she asked and Marek rose to his feet, scooping up Noah to hold him. When the baby held his arms out to Camille, she took him.

"Ashley left for the evening. Told us to not wait up. I told her we wouldn't," Marek said in a husky tone. "I have plans for you."

"I can't wait. But I do have to feed this fellow or no one will do anything else and he'll still be awake when we go to bed."

"When we go to bed," Marek repeated. "I can't wait. Let's feed the hungry boy."

"I agree."

It was nine o'clock when they were in their room and finally alone. Marek drew Camille into his embrace. One look in his dark eyes and her heart began to race. "I've waited all day for this moment," he whispered and kissed away her answer.

Her heart thudded. Each time they made love, he became more important to her. In the throes of passion, she had whispered her declaration of love, but he had never heard her and she intended to keep it that way until she heard words of love cross his lips.

She poured out her passion as they made love far into the night. Holding him tightly, she ran one hand down his bare back as he lowered himself between her legs and slowly filled her, taking time to heighten tension, making her want him desperately as she arched beneath him and then rocked with him. "I love you," she cried, unable to hold back, certain he hadn't heard her as it had always been.

She held him as his control vanished and he thrust swiftly, taking her over an edge. "Marek," she cried, grasping his solid body as if he were the only anchor in her life.

"Camille," he ground out her name while he shuddered in his climax. "I love you."

Her eyes flew open. Moving with him, she held him. Had she imagined his declaration? She had dreamed of it too many times to count. Passion drove away her questions and she rocked with him, united physically, her heart belonging to him totally.

When he finally held her in his arms as legs were entwined and her black hair spilled over his shoulder, he showered her with light kisses. "I love you, Camille."

She gazed into his dark eyes while her heart missed beats. "You really mean that?" she whispered.

"Yes," he said gruffly, gazing at her solemnly. He brushed long strands of her hair away from her face. "Love may complicate our life."

"Never. This is better. I love you and I've loved you since before we said wedding vows."

He stared at her intently. "Why didn't you tell me?"

She shook her head. "You weren't ready."

He stared at her again in silence, and she wondered what he was thinking. "I'm ready now," he whispered and kissed her hard, holding her against his heart while joy filled her.

"Wait," he said, turning to open a drawer in the bedside table. "This is for you."

Surprised, she glanced from the package to him, and then she took it to untie a blue ribbon and tear away the wrapper. She opened the box to take out a black velvet box. When she opened it, she gasped as the sapphire and diamond necklace caught the light.

"This is magnificent. It's stunning," she said, sitting up and pulling the sheet beneath her arms.

"Here's what is stunning," he said, sitting up to fasten it around her neck.

"Marek, thank you. This is the most beautiful jewelry I've ever owned except my wedding ring, which is gorgeous."

"I love you, Camille," he said again and kissed her.

Her heart pounded wildly, more from his declaration of love than the necklace which had taken her breath at first sight.

He paused. "We can make this a complete, real marriage. If we both love each other. Have you thought about the possibility of scaling back your career?"

Startled, she frowned. "No, I haven't. My career doesn't diminish my love for you or Noah. I don't want to scale back or give it up. I can't do that. I feel I can achieve so much more, and I love opera. I live and breathe opera. But it doesn't take away from the love I feel for you."

They stared at each other and she hurt, with a knot tightening inside. A muscle worked in his jaw as he stared intently at her. She had no idea what he was thinking.

"I don't know about our future. I do know about now," he said gruffly, reaching for her to pull her into his embrace.

She wrapped her arms around him and let her love for him pour into her lovemaking.

They loved far into the night again and early the next morning he left for the ranch to get out of her way and return to his own work. As she showered and dressed, she thought about his impossible request, his declaration of love that obviously had a stipulation. She didn't know if that would cause him to end this marriage of convenience or give it less time and attention. Whatever happened, she couldn't turn her back on her career now.

Saturday Marek had to stay at the ranch because of a crisis on a neighboring ranch where the barn caught on fire and two trucks burned. Marek loaned a truck to the neighbor and tried to help any way he could, but by the time he returned to his ranch and had cleaned up, Camille said she was exhausted and going to bed early, so he decided to fly to Dallas on Sunday.

She had a rehearsal on Sunday and a costume fitting that had been unexpected. Once again, it was late when she was finally free and they ate a cold dinner at ten.

The weekend was too short. The next week Marek mulled over the prospects of their married life. He hated being away from her. He loved her, and, as time went by, he knew that love would grow until it was as strong as the oaks that grew at his ranch.

What could he do to keep them together?

The phone rang, interrupting his thoughts, and he answered to hear his sister. "I was calling to tell you we are all excited about Camille's performance. The girls are deliriously happy to be going and this will definitely be their first opera. It's my first and Frank's and I suspect it's yours."

"I've seen bits and pieces, at an event years ago."

"No doubt some beautiful woman talked you into it. We're thrilled to get to keep Noah opening night so Ashley can attend with her family."

"It's good for him to spend time with your family and Ashley is happy to be going with her family."

"You don't sound happy. Is everything all right?" Before

he could answer, she continued, "You're in love with her, aren't you?"

"Ginny, stop being big sis for a few minutes."

"Impossible," she replied. "I'm sorry. Take care of yourself."

"At least you didn't say, 'I told you so.' I thank you for that."

"I won't say any more on the subject, but I'm here if you want to talk."

"Thanks."

"I'll call Camille about Noah."

He heard the click and she was gone. He felt torn between the heartache of loving Camille and living this way or ending this paper marriage or trying to get her to give up her career. Of all his choices, ending the marriage was not tolerable. He loved her even if he was going to get hurt again as much as he had been hurt over losing Jillian. Why was love such a risk?

He would go to opening night and then for two weeks, he would see almost nothing of her. What kind of incentive could he offer to get her to cut back a little?

For her opening night performance, he had no intention of doing anything to take away the glory of that moment from her.

Ten

The following night Marek sat in the box Camille had arranged. He was with the Avanoles. Her parents, her brother and both sisters were present. Marek thought he should have gone sooner to hear her sing. He had heard her sing scales and practice exercises, but nothing else.

When the conductor appeared and the orchestra commenced playing, Marek's mind was on Camille and when he would be alone with her, something he didn't expect to happen until this opera ended its last performance. And then Camille came onstage and his attention went to her. She had told him the story, which sounded sad and gloomy with death for her character at the end.

As she sang, Marek was mesmerized. He had heard her practice, but he had never been in the room with her. Now the full richness of her voice filled the opera house.

Chills ran down his spine. He knew nothing about opera. He had seen singers on television performing bits, but never a whole opera, never in person. Camille's voice soared, filling the opera house with purest sound.

He was transfixed, steeped in the crystal sounds of her voice. She stopped and in minutes the music started again and then her golden voice with its astonishing range.

Her acting was lively and vivacious as he had expected, while her singing captured his heart. He would remember this night the rest of his life.

She was meant to sing. She had a true talent and his heart felt as if it were breaking into a million pieces. Even though he knew nothing about opera, there was no mistaking that she had incredible talent. This went beyond their two lives. This was a talent that should be shared.

All this time he had had no idea how gifted she was.

Press releases and media could be filled with exaggerated hype, fed by agents, luck, friendships and the views of the reporter. Her voice flew beyond all those things. No one could question her tone, range or ability.

In a moment of clarity, he saw he could never take her from the stage. Her voice was meant for the famous opera, meant for the world to hear.

She belonged to her talent and she needed to give herself to the public because her gift was awesome.

He stopped thinking and listened to her clear soprano as she sang. He hurt with an incredible pain. How could he have done this to himself again? He couldn't ask her to compromise, so perhaps he was going to have to, in order for them to have a bearable marriage.

Music filled the room, like sunshine surrounding him, while at the same time he felt as if he were tumbling into the darkness of another lost love, of pain and separation because he loved her. She had captured his heart and he had enabled her to do so.

He wondered at the perverseness of humans as he shifted

restlessly, because for the first time in his life, he had met a woman he couldn't love on his own terms.

Dazed, hurting while at the same time spellbound by her singing, he sat through the opera, applauding, calling "Brava" with others and knowing she was lost to him. He could never try to win her away from the life she had been destined to live.

He went through the motions, talking to her family.

Camille had an opening night party for the cast. Families were invited. Backstage, he stood to one side to let others surround her to talk to her. She was radiant, smiling constantly, and she looked more gorgeous than ever.

His pain increased as he watched her and saw what he was losing. There was absolutely no possibility of his having more than a fraction of her life. He thought of the new ring he had bought for her, to give her as a token of his love for her. He loved her, but he would not take her from her career and he would not give her that ring.

Her family was staying with them, so he wasn't alone with her until one in the morning when they finally closed the bedroom door. Her black hair was partially braided and fastened on her head. The remaining locks fell freely across her back. Her makeup was thick, dramatic, emphasizing her large, expressive eyes and full mouth, making her breathtakingly beautiful. She smiled in triumph at him.

"You have a fantastic voice," he said, crossing the room to place his hands on her shoulders. "You belong onstage, Camille. I've become an opera fan."

"I'm so glad. So happy," she said, hugging him and standing on tiptoe to kiss him.

Desire consumed him. He needed her kisses, her love on this night. He knew he would lose her in the future, but tonight she was in his arms, radiant from performing and her success. He tightened his arms around her and kissed her hard, wanting to hold her, love her and make her want to stay in his arms forever. For a few hours, he would cling to a dream that had no substance, but would give him joy tonight.

Later, when she was stretched against him, she chatted and finally raised herself slightly on her elbow to look at him. "Why so quiet tonight?"

She met a dark, impenetrable gaze. "I hadn't thought that much about your voice and your singing," he answered finally. "You have a true and beautiful talent. Your voice is wonderful. You'll be a star and it will take you far from here."

"I'll always be able to come home."

"That's right. But you'll also always have to leave to go perform somewhere."

"This shouldn't interfere with you and it may actually give you more time with Noah. Besides, at this point it is sheer speculation. I have a long way to go to become that kind of star."

"I have a feeling it will come much faster than you think."

"I think you're biased, but I hope you're right. I'm overjoyed you liked the opera."

Camille's *La Traviata* performance had been a triumph and the time had flown. Now as she sat on a Rangel jet bound for Santa Fe, she glanced next to her at Marek, who was poring over Noah's baby book.

Marek's thick black lashes were dark shadows above his cheeks. A stray lock of hair curled on his forehead. He had withdrawn into a shell the past few days, and she had wondered what had triggered it. Was it something in his life or had it been the interference of her performance and the intense practice beforehand?

"What? You have the intense look of a cat ready to pounce on prey."

"How'd you know that?" she asked.

"I can tell," he answered casually, closing the baby book to hand it back to her. "Nice. You need a picture of Kern. I'll get you one."

"I'd like that."

"Now, why the intense examination?" he repeated.

She could feel heat fill her cheeks. "You've changed and I was trying to figure why. You're preoccupied."

"Business," he said. In the time she had known Marek, she had never seen him concerned about business problems or ranch problems. Jess bore the brunt of those. Marek had a shuttered look and she couldn't glean anything from his expression.

"I don't think that's really the answer," she said, letting it drop for now until they were alone. They were flying to Santa Fe to get a place to live and then she would leave Dallas. Was it the move that had him on edge?

She was amazed how fast and efficient Marek was when they arrived in Santa Fe and later when she went through the move. She had another opera performance to prepare for, and they agreed he would leave Noah with her in Santa Fe and he would return to the ranch until opening night.

When she told him goodbye at the airport in New Mexico, he held her tightly and kissed her until she was breathless, her heart racing, and she didn't want him to stop.

He released her abruptly. "Better go," he said gruffly, his gaze trailing over her features as if memorizing them. When he turned away to board the jet and she left to go back to a waiting limo Marek had arranged for her while she was in Santa Fe, she had a distinct feeling something was amiss.

Getting up before sunrise, working until dark at any physical labor he could find, Marek threw himself into work at the ranch. He hated being alone in the house, trying to keep books, because his mind would wander constantly to Camille. He missed her and he missed Noah. He talked to Camille each day and saw them on Skype and tried to keep a fragile contact, but she was busy getting ready to perform Pamina in *The Magic Flute,* and Noah couldn't converse with him. When he saw them on Skype, he hurt badly, wanting her, loving her, but hating the separation. He missed Noah's happy little face.

Instead of growing accustomed to being away from her, to seeing her on opening night and when the performance was over, he hurt more with Camille and Noah out of his life and getting only tiny glimpses and contacts with them.

The last week in August he had to be in Dallas for a Rangel Foundation meeting, and Ginny had asked him to lunch beforehand. He listened to her chatter about the girls and saw their latest pictures.

"I haven't seen them for too long, Ginny. Bring them to the ranch this weekend so they can ride."

"I will accept that invitation," she said over a crisp green salad while Marek ate only a few bites of his onion burger. "You miss Camille, don't you?"

"Camille and Noah. Yes," he said, giving her a steady look. "Want to hear you were right?"

"No, I don't. I don't want you hurt, and you've lost weight and look like you haven't slept for weeks. Maybe you should go see her more."

Marek shook his head. "I'm in the way when she practices or has lessons. She's busy when she's getting ready to perform and when she's performing."

"I can imagine, but you can't keep on like this."

"I know, Ginny," he said, looking away and she let the subject drop.

Through the meeting Marek thought about the future. He flew back to the ranch, the one haven in his life and now even the ranch seemed empty and hurtful.

That evening Jess appeared at the back door with a six-pack of cold beer. "Want company?"

Marek smiled slightly. "Hell, yes. I can use some company, Jess. Beer looks good, too. Come on in."

Jess's boot heels clicked against bare floorboards as he headed to the kitchen. In minutes they sat at the kitchen table while silence stretched between them.

"Camille was meant for opera. I can't take her from that because she has the talent to be a star."

After another stretch of silence, Marek ran his finger along the cold bottle. "Maybe I've been looking for what I had with Jillian, but Camille is different. I can't expect her to give me what I expected with Jillian. Camille has all this talent. I'm going to have to settle for being a small part of her life, something I'm not used to doing."

"If you love her and that's what it takes, that's a good decision," Jess said. "I'd give anything for a small part of my family."

"You're right, Jess. I suppose it's because I'm not used to being the one who compromises."

"I don't think you are."

"For Camille, I'm willing to try to make this marriage work."

"If you love her, that's a good solution. You'll do what you have to. So will she. You won't lose Noah. What boy wouldn't want to come to the ranch?"

"Might be a few, particularly one who's raised backstage at operas."

"You'll see," Jess said, and Marek felt a degree better. His cell rang. "That's her, Jess."

"Go ahead. I'll head home anyway. Keep the beer for next time," Jess said, standing and picking up his hat to go while Marek answered his phone. His heart missed a beat when he heard Camille's voice.

* * *

After talking for over an hour to Marek, Camille lay in bed and contemplated her future. She loved Marek and she didn't think she would ever love again. Life without him looked unbelievably empty. What did she want in her future? Would it matter to him what she wanted? One time he had asked her about scaling back her career, and she couldn't. The last time they had been together, he had seemed restrained, preoccupied, yet their lovemaking had grown better and more passionate each time they were together.

What did she want in the future for herself? As his wife, money was no longer in the equation. Did she want to sing for the thrill and enjoyment of it? For the success? It was grinding work—voice and language lessons, daily voice practice, studying operas and arias, working out. She had Noah to consider. What did she want for her future?

She wanted Marek in her life and Noah's. She wanted another baby. She also wanted to sing at La Scala and to reach a pinnacle in opera where she became a name.

Tears flowed freely and she turned, burying her face in her pillow to cry silently. She wanted it all—the best of both worlds, her love, her baby and her career. What did she want to sacrifice?

All the time Camille was in Saint Louis, she thought about her future. At night she sat up long hours, staring out the window at the familiar yard where she had grown up. What did she want most of all? Marek couldn't make that decision for her. That one she had to make herself.

Making her decision, she cut her visit home short by two days and returned to Dallas, calling Marek and telling him she knew what she wanted to do.

Eleven

When Marek met her at the airport, as arranged earlier, they took Noah to Ginny's before going to Marek's Dallas house.

Struggling to wait to hold and kiss her, Marek finally placed his hands on her waist and took another long look at her, relishing every moment of having her with him. In a clinging, low-cut black dress that ended above her knees, she looked breathtaking. Her hair was pinned up on the sides, hanging free in the back. While it was gorgeous, he longed to take it down. Take down her hair, kiss her, seduce her and spend the rest of the day and night in bed making love.

"You can't imagine how much I've missed you," he said, kissing her passionately.

Minutes later, she leaned away to frame his face with her hands. "You haven't seemed as happy lately. I didn't want to talk about it over the phone. I wanted to wait until we were together."

"I couldn't be happier now that you're in my arms," he whispered, kissing her throat.

"Marek, listen a minute." He raised his head to focus on her.

"You asked me some time ago to scale back my career, and I told you I couldn't. Things haven't been quite the same between us since."

"I've had a lot of time to think about that. You were meant to share your talent. I love you and I'll settle for the time I can have with you."

"You mean that?" she asked, her eyes growing huge.

"I mean it. Even if it's just a little of your time. I love you. I need you in my life. I need to know that I have your love."

Smiling, with a sparkle coming to her blue eyes, she kissed him passionately again. His hands wound in her hair as he kissed her in return, and then his arm circled her waist to hold her tightly.

She finally leaned away. "That thrills me, that you are willing to make such a sacrifice for me."

"You don't know how much I love you," he said, desire a smoldering fire in him.

"Marek, while we were apart, I gave thought to what I want to do. You think my life should be opera. I'm not the only singer—not even remotely. As your wife, my earnings no longer are part of this."

"That's beside the point."

"Not when my family needed my help and I had to count on my voice. I still want success in opera. Specifically, I want the lead in an opera at the Metropolitan. I want the lead at La Scala."

"You should be the lead both places," he said, his voice thickening. He could inhale the scent of her perfume, feel her narrow waist beneath his hands. They stood with only inches separating them. "I also want the love of the man I love," she said in a throaty voice as tears filled her eyes. "I want Noah to have a family. I want him to have two siblings. I want a family."

"I want you to have both," Marek whispered. "I want you to have it all. Everything possible to make you happy."

"I love you," she said, gazing solemnly at him. "Listen a moment. Here's my plan." Her voice strengthened, and she poked his chest with her forefinger as if she needed to get his attention. "Give me three years. I'm only twenty-five. For the next three years put up with the separations and the inconveniences and let me pursue my career totally. In three years, I will retire. Noah will still be in preschool, a little boy, not too old for siblings."

"In three—"

"Do not interrupt until I'm through," she said, startling him. "I will want to give it up in three years. I've thought this through carefully. I know you thought you had our marriage all mapped out and it would work and then it didn't. I'm sure that I don't want to pursue my career for years. I want my family. I want your love. I love you and I'm not giving you up just because you're shocked by my talent and think I should give up everything for my career. Occasionally in your life, you're wrong. Can you give me three years if I give you the rest?"

Stunned, he stared at her while he thought about what she proposed.

"Marek, for heaven's sake. I love you," she cried, standing on tiptoe to kiss him.

Marek's resistance to her kiss disappeared. His arms locked tightly around her and he kissed her, letting go all the longing he had bottled up since hearing her perform. As if a dam had burst, desire poured over him, making him shake with urgency. He wanted her desperately and everything else vanished.

Oblivious of her hands moving over him, he unzipped her dress. She fumbled with his shirt and he yanked it off, popping buttons and sending them flying while she shook out of her dress and let it fall.

In minutes he picked her up to love her while they kissed and her long legs were locked around him. She was soft, a flame burning away all hurt. He loved her wildly, wanting to hold her forever in his arms.

When she finally clung to him, relaxing against him, he let her slide to put her feet on the floor. She glanced up.

"I think you've already given me your answer. Right?"

That night in his bed, he held her close as he toyed with long locks of her raven hair. "We'll follow your plan, Camille," he said. "In three years, you may change—"

She placed her fingers lightly on his mouth while she shook her head. "No. I adore Noah. I want a family. I love you and want your love. With the money you have, I can continue to have voice lessons and sing in local events in Dallas or Houston or even New Mexico, maybe once a year or less. We'll see, but I'm sure I will not continue with this all-consuming career that takes everything."

"You don't have to talk me into it. For better or worse, I'm accepting your idea," he said happily.

Smiling, she rolled over to trail feather kisses on his cheek and jaw, down over his shoulder. "If I get my wish about the Met and La Scala in less than three years, we can move up that timetable."

He laughed, a deep rumbling sound that vibrated in his chest. "Wait a minute."

Turning, he opened a drawer in a bedside table. He settled back to take her right hand in his.

"Camille, you've given me my full life back. You've given me Noah. You've given me love. Your wedding ring was a token of our contract and agreement to marry for Noah. This ring is a token of my gratitude and all my love," he said in a husky voice. He dropped a small package in her lap.

She blinked and looked up at him, seeing warmth and love in his eyes. Her heart thudded over his declaration. Tearing away wrappings, she opened her gift. With a racing pulse, she raised the lid to see a dazzling diamond ring.

"Marek, it's beautiful," she said, throwing her arms around his neck. "I am overjoyed."

He smiled at her. "I'll do everything in my power to keep you happy."

"Including coming to Budapest part of the time with me, even though I'll be busy."

"Including going to Hungary part of the time," he answered, smiling with her. "Whatever I can do to keep your love, keep you happy, keep you and Noah in my life however much or little that turns out to be."

Joy shook her and tears of happiness spilled. Before he could say anything more, she kissed him, knowing his love and being a family for Noah was what she wanted more than all else.

* * * * *

COMING NEXT MONTH from Harlequin Desire®
AVAILABLE JUNE 4, 2013

#2233 SUNSET SEDUCTION
The Slades of Sunset Ranch
Charlene Sands
When the chance to jump into bed with longtime crush Lucas Slade comes along, Audrey Thomas can't help but seize it. Now the tricky part is to wrangle her way into the rich rancher's *heart*.

#2234 AFFAIRS OF STATE
Daughters of Power: The Capital
Jennifer Lewis
Can Ariella Winthrop—revealed as the secret love child of the U.S. president—find love with a royal prince whose family disapproves of her illegitimacy?

#2235 HIS FOR THE TAKING
Rich, Rugged Ranchers
Ann Major
It's been six years since Maddie Gray left town in disgrace. But now she's back, and wealthy rancher John Coleman can't stay away from the lover who once betrayed him.

#2236 TAMING THE LONE WOLFF
The Men of Wolff Mountain
Janice Maynard
Security expert Larkin Wolff lives by a code, but when he's hired to protect an innocent heiress, he's tempted to break all his rules and become *personally* involved with his client....

#2237 HOLLYWOOD HOUSE CALL
Jules Bennett
When an accident forces receptionist Callie Matthews to move in with her boss, her relationship with the sexy doctor becomes much less about business and *very* much about pleasure....

#2238 THE FIANCÉE CHARADE
The Pearl House
Fiona Brand
Faced with losing custody of her daughter, Gemma O'Neill will do anything—even pretend to be engaged to the man who fathered her child.

HDCNM0513

REQUEST YOUR FREE BOOKS!
2 FREE NOVELS PLUS 2 FREE GIFTS!

HARLEQUIN *Desire*

ALWAYS POWERFUL, PASSIONATE AND PROVOCATIVE

YES! Please send me 2 FREE Harlequin Desire® novels and my 2 FREE gifts (gifts are worth about $10). After receiving them, if I don't wish to receive any more books, I can return the shipping statement marked "cancel." If I don't cancel, I will receive 6 brand-new novels every month and be billed just $4.55 per book in the U.S. or $4.99 per book in Canada. That's a savings of at least 13% off the cover price! It's quite a bargain! Shipping and handling is just 50¢ per book in the U.S. and 75¢ per book in Canada.* I understand that accepting the 2 free books and gifts places me under no obligation to buy anything. I can always return a shipment and cancel at any time. Even if I never buy another book, the two free books and gifts are mine to keep forever.

225/326 HDN F4ZC

Name _____ (PLEASE PRINT) _____

Address _____ Apt. #

City _____ State/Prov. _____ Zip/Postal Code

Signature (if under 18, a parent or guardian must sign)

Mail to the **Harlequin® Reader Service:**
IN U.S.A.: P.O. Box 1867, Buffalo, NY 14240-1867
IN CANADA: P.O. Box 609, Fort Erie, Ontario L2A 5X3

Want to try two free books from another line?
Call 1-800-873-8635 or visit www.ReaderService.com.

* Terms and prices subject to change without notice. Prices do not include applicable taxes. Sales tax applicable in N.Y. Canadian residents will be charged applicable taxes. Offer not valid in Quebec. This offer is limited to one order per household. Not valid for current subscribers to Harlequin Desire books. All orders subject to credit approval. Credit or debit balances in a customer's account(s) may be offset by any other outstanding balance owed by or to the customer. Please allow 4 to 6 weeks for delivery. Offer available while quantities last.

Your Privacy—The Harlequin® Reader Service is committed to protecting your privacy. Our Privacy Policy is available online at www.ReaderService.com or upon request from the Harlequin Reader Service.

We make a portion of our mailing list available to reputable third parties that offer products we believe may interest you. If you prefer that we not exchange your name with third parties, or if you wish to clarify or modify your communication preferences, please visit us at www.ReaderService.com/consumerschoice or write to us at Harlequin Reader Service Preference Service, P.O. Box 9062, Buffalo, NY 14269. Include your complete name and address.

HD13R

SPECIAL EXCERPT FROM

HARLEQUIN®

$\mathcal{D}esire$

presents

SUNSET SEDUCTION

The latest installment of USA TODAY *bestselling author*

Charlene Sands's miniseries

THE SLADES OF SUNSET RANCH

All grown up, Audrey Faith Thomas seizes her chance to act on a teenage crush. Now she must face the consequences....

U*sually* not much unnerved Audrey Faith Thomas, except for the time when her big brother was bucked off Old Stormy at an Amarillo rodeo and broke his back.

Audrey shuddered at the memory and thanked the Almighty that Casey was alive and well and bossy as ever. But as she sat behind the wheel of her car, driving toward her fate, the fear coursing through her veins had nothing to do with her brother's disastrous five-second ride. This fear was much different. It made her want to turn her Chevy pickup truck around and go home to Reno and forget all about showing up at Sunset Ranch unannounced.

To face Lucas Slade.

The man she'd seduced and then abandoned in the middle of the night.

Audrey swallowed hard. She still couldn't believe what she'd done.

Last month, after an argument and a three week standoff with her brother, she'd ventured to his Lake Tahoe cabin to make amends. He'd been right about the boyfriend she'd just dumped and she'd needed Casey's strong shoulder to cry on.

The last person she'd expected to find there was Luke Slade—the man she'd measured every other man against—sleeping in the guest room bed, *her bed*. Luke was the guy she'd crushed on during her teen years while traveling the rodeo circuit with Casey.

Seeing him had sent all rational thoughts flying out the window. This was her chance. She wouldn't let her prudish upbringing interfere with what she needed. When he rasped, "Come closer," in the darkened room, she'd taken that as an invitation to climb into bed with him, consequences be damned.

Well…she'd gotten a lot more than a shoulder to cry on, and it had been glorious.

Now she would finally come face-to-face with Luke. She'd confront him about the night they'd shared and confess her love for him, if it came down to that. She wondered what he thought about her abandoning him that night.

She would soon find out.

Find out what happens when Audrey and Luke reunite in

SUNSET SEDUCTION
by Charlene Sands.

Available June 2013 from Harlequin® Desire®
wherever books are sold!

HARLEQUIN®

A *Romance* FOR EVERY MOOD™

Love the Harlequin book you just read?

Your opinion matters.

Review this book on your favorite book site, review site, blog or your own social media properties and share your opinion with other readers!

Be sure to connect with us at:
Harlequin.com/Newsletters
Facebook.com/HarlequinBooks
Twitter.com/HarlequinBooks

HARLEQUIN®

A *Romance* FOR EVERY MOOD™

Stay up-to-date on all your
romance-reading news with the
Harlequin Shopping Guide,
featuring bestselling authors, exciting new
miniseries, books to watch and more!

The newest issue will be delivered right to you
with our compliments! There are 4 each year.

Signing up is easy.

EMAIL

ShoppingGuide@Harlequin.ca

WRITE TO US

HARLEQUIN BOOKS
Attention: Customer Service Department
P.O. Box 9057, Buffalo, NY 14269-9057

OR PHONE

1-800-873-8635 in the United States
1-888-343-9777 in Canada

Please allow 4-6 weeks for delivery of the first issue by mail.

HSGSIGNUP

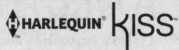

Revenge and seduction intertwine…

Andreas Xenakis has never forgiven or forgotten
Siena DePiero. And when she becomes destitute after
her family fortune disappears, he makes her an offer
she can't afford to refuse: become his lover/mistress,
for a price.

Andreas has waited years to get his revenge,
but one night with beautiful Siena shatters his
poor-little-rich-girl illusions and unleashes a passion
that only a lifetime together might be able to sate…
if he can convince her to stay.

FORGIVEN BUT NOT FORGOTTEN?

by *USA TODAY* bestselling author

Abby Green

**Available May 21, 2013
wherever books are sold!**

www.Harlequin.com

HP13154